The Running Back

Robert McKay

THE RUNNING BACK

Harcourt Brace Jovanovich

New York and London

F
M

Requests for permission to make copies of any part
of the work should be mailed to:
Permissions, Harcourt Brace Jovanovich, Inc.,
757 Third Avenue, New York, N.Y. 10017

Printed in the United States of America

Library of Congress Cataloging in Publication Data

McKay, Robert, 1921–
The running back.

SUMMARY: An 18-year-old goes from a reformatory to
a small town high school, joins the football team, and
tries to put his life in order.
[1. Football—Fiction] I. Title.
PZ7.M1914Ru   [Fic.]   79-87523
ISBN 0-15-269782-9

First edition

BCDEFGHIJK

To John Garvey
and to John Groninger
and to Margaret Hammond
and to other friends who helped

The dice of God are always loaded.

—Ralph Waldo Emerson

The Running Back

1

When I got home from school that day, Aunt Frieda gave me a sidelong glance. "You're pretty late, Jack," she said, with a little question in it.

Aunt Frieda was okay. But she was a worrier, and no matter how hard she tried to let me know that the past was over and done with, I always knew there were things on her mind, things she couldn't forget about.

"I know." I opened the refrigerator door and poured myself a glass of milk. "I was watching football practice."

"Oh? I thought you weren't interested in football anymore." Her blue eyes were crinkled and her mouth a little uncertain. Although my aunt Frieda was fifty years old, you'd never know it. She looked about thirty-five. Her husband, my uncle Fred, was the same age and looked closer to sixty. White hair, big belly, slow moving. I'd only been living with them for a month now and I still wasn't totally at ease with them, or they with me, but we were getting along better than I ever used to think I'd get along with anybody.

"Well, look . . . maybe I'm changing my mind. Would it be okay with you if I went out for the team?"

"Of course, it would! I think it'd be just fine!" Aunt Frieda was a very emotional woman. For a minute I thought she was going to burst out crying.

"Hey, boy, I'm all for it!" Uncle Fred beamed when I mentioned it to him at supper. Uncle Fred owned the only hardware store in Holbrook. Medium-sized store in a small town. It hadn't made him rich by any means. But it had given him a kind of solid-citizen reputation or image that he relished. Everybody knew him. Maybe they didn't all like him—sometimes he was grumpy and outspoken— but they knew him and respected him.

Right now he was concentrating on his pot roast and candied carrots and mashed potatoes, but his brow was starting to wrinkle. And I had already learned that when the brow started to wrinkle, Uncle Fred was having a thought. Or, more likely, a second thought.

"You know, there's one thing, Jack," he said, putting his fork down on his plate and looking at me like a white-headed old owl. "You're a big kid and you might be a good football player for all I know. But . . . well. . . ." He fumbled around for a minute. "I just think you oughtn't to get your hopes too high. These boys in Holbrook have had the benefit of real good coaching, and you just startin' out in your senior year and all . . . well, what I'm tryin' to say is, if you don't make the team you shouldn't get all shook up or anything. You understand what I'm saying?"

"Sure. I'm just going to give it a try, that's all."

"Good boy!" He went back to his pot roast with an uncreased brow.

It had all started the day before, when Mr. Foss, who taught algebra and also coached the football team, stopped me in the hall.

"Ever play any football, Jack?"

"Oh . . . some."

"What position?"

"Mostly running back."

"Why don't you come out for the team? We could sure use some help in the backfield."

"Well. . . ." I hesitated. "I guess I really don't want to play. I'm not that good, anyway."

Mr. Foss looked at me, his face serious. I didn't know him very well, but after sitting in his class for two weeks I was starting to think he was a pretty good guy.

"Listen. Will you do me a favor?"

"Depends."

He grinned. He was a big man, over six feet, around forty years old, getting a little thick in the middle and thin on top.

"Nothing heavy," he said. "Will you stop by my room this afternoon? Promise I won't keep you more than fifteen minutes."

I felt a touch of the old anger or resentment or panic or whatever it was. But then I told myself to cut it out. He was either going to try to talk me into playing football or give me a little hell about my work. I'd never taken algebra before, and I was having trouble with it. So I told him okay, I'd see him after school.

When I came into his room he was standing by the window, hands deep in the pockets of the baggy corduroy pants he always wore.

"Hi." He gave me his usual serious nod. Then he turned one of the student desk-chairs around and sat down, so he was facing me. I sat down, too, but I didn't turn my chair around and I left a row between us.

"Pretty cautious, aren't you?"

I started to get a feeling of what was coming.

"That was exactly the kind of thing I didn't want to say." He scratched hard at the top of his balding head. "You've got to make allowances for me, Jack. Seems I've always got my foot in my mouth, one way or another. Probably one of the reasons I'm still coaching football at a hick school like this."

That surprised me. Holbrook High *was* kind of a hick school, at least in my opinion, but it was very strong on school spirit and I never expected to hear the coach call it a hick school.

"I'll just come straight to the point," he said. "It's the only way I can do things." Then he stopped and gazed at me for a long minute or two.

"Jack, I know all about you. No, of course not *all* about you, but about Marshfield and some of the things that happened before that."

"Yeah? When I started school here, the principal told me nobody'd find out a damn thing. Guess he meant just the first two weeks."

Mr. Foss frowned and scratched his head again. "This is a small town, Jack. I don't know how stories get out, but they do. Have you been getting any flak from anybody . . . the other kids . . . teachers?"

"No. More like the opposite. People bending over backward. At first I thought maybe I was being a little paranoid about it."

"Jack, I don't want to sound preachy, but you've got to remember that you did commit burglary, and you were convicted and served time for it. No Brinks job, sure . . . and maybe there were extenuating circumstances, but . . . well. . . . If this were a big city school, nobody'd bother bending either way. I taught a couple of years in Cleveland, and sometimes it seemed like half the kids in my classes were on probation."

"I'm not on probation."

"I know. I know. But most of the kids around here—teachers too—don't know anything about a place like Marshfield, except for some of the wild stuff they see on

TV. So they're curious and cautious and probably just don't know what to do."

"Look, they don't have to do anything. All I want is to be left alone, so I can get through this year and graduate."

"You sure that's all you want? Being left alone is not exactly the greatest thing in the world, either, you know. Why don't you come out for the team? Give yourself a chance and give the school a chance. Corny as it sounds, you might find something good happening . . . both ways."

"I don't know. I'll think about it."

"Yeah, you'll think about it." He was scowling at the floor. I started to get up. "Wait a minute. I'm going to tell you something that'll probably make you mad, but I'm going to tell you anyway. Two days ago I talked to Chuck Grossman on the phone."

"You got no right to be checkin' up on me!"

"I wasn't checking up, not like you mean. Now sit still a minute and let me talk. For the past two weeks I've seen you doing laps on the track, always alone. I've seen the way you run, the way you move. Now I know something about athletes, and if you're not a natural there never was one. Okay. . . ." He paused and took a breath. "Maybe I should have talked to you first. But you see, I played football with Chuck Grossman at Ohio State. So talking to him was not like calling some stranger and asking questions about you. I just wanted to know if you'd played any ball down there, and if you were as good as I thought you might be."

I wasn't looking at him. Everything inside me was whirling again. Chuck Grossman. The only real human good person I had known at Marshfield. I remembered the way it had been, the practices and then the games, when for an hour or so I could almost forget where I was.

"You know what he told me?"

I didn't answer.

"He told me you were as good as I thought you might be."

Finally I turned and looked at him. "So what does that mean?"

"What're you—six-one, hundred and seventy?"

"Around there."

"By the time you're twenty you'll be an inch or two taller and probably go two hundred, maybe more. You've got big bones."

"So?"

"So you've got the equipment. You've got the talent. There's not one boy in a thousand with your potential. Don't throw it away."

I folded my arms across my chest and stared at the desk top. I knew what he was saying. Had already said it to myself enough times. But there were other sides to the story, too, and sometimes it was like a war, the different sides all fighting each other, inside me.

"Are you afraid to try to be the best?"

"Oh, hell." I stood up. "Maybe I am. I already tried it a few times." I started for the door.

"Try it again," Mr. Foss said quietly. "It might be a little different here."

I stopped at the door, looked over my shoulder at him. Mr. Foss doesn't look anything like Chuck Grossman, but just for an instant there he looked a lot like him.

After thinking about it that night and the next day and then watching the team practice, I decided to give it a try. Watching the practice was what really did it. The huff and the snap and the hits and, most of all, the pure motion. The running, that's what got me.

My first day's practice turned out to be not so much. After some calisthenics and grass drills and a few trips around the field with the blocking sled, the rest of the team split up into groups to work on offense, defense, man-to-man contact, whatever they needed.

But not me. First I had to get outfitted, which took some time. I mean finding the right pads, the right fit in everything, which is important if you don't plan to get hurt. I finally got suited up and it was pretty much okay, except I couldn't find any 11-A shoes. The assistant coach, a young guy named Eakins, said their budget was tighter than some of the shoes, but he'd try to order me a pair. Then he took me out on the field (in my 11-Ds) and I spent the rest of the afternoon running laps, doing wind sprints, grass drills, calisthenics, and all the tiresome stuff that goes under the general heading of GETTING IN SHAPE.

On top of that, I had to stay after practice every day the first week for an extra half-hour's skull session with Coach Foss. Of course, I didn't know anything about Holbrook's offensive system, and it can take time to learn a new playbook, especially if it's based on something complicated like, say, a wishbone, and you've never played the wishbone.

But this time it turned out to be no problem. Foss ran his team pretty much the same way Chuck Grossman had run his at Marshfield. Mostly straight-ahead, old-fashioned football. Probably because both had played under Woody Hayes at Ohio State.

"Maybe if I could find a high school quarterback who could read defenses, throw strikes, and keep his cool . . . maybe then I'd go to more of a passing game," Coach Foss told me. "Now Benny Younger has a hell of an arm and can hit a target, too . . . but he never knows what the defense is doing. I think he's got tunnel vision."

9

I was surprised, the coach talking to me like this, but then I figured he was just trying to build my confidence, make me feel at home. The more I saw of him, the more he reminded me of Chuck Grossman. My first two years at Marshfield had been pretty rough. And if it hadn't been for Grossman, the last two years might have been even worse.

I was a wise young punk fresh off the streets of Cleveland.

What we used to do, me and three or four like me, was rob stores for the big guys. Burglarize, not rob. I mean that's the way the law sees it. Robbery is when you take something away from somebody by force or by putting fear into them. Burglary is when you sneak into some place and steal the stuff and nobody knows you're there. You hope.

The big guys used to plan the jobs. The big guys in the Sabers were maybe sixteen to eighteen years old. They'd pick out a store and watch it and make sure it didn't have a burglar alarm, or if it did they'd disconnect it, and then find a way for us to get in. Maybe open a window from the inside in the daytime. Different things. Then they'd send us stupid punks out on a certain night to do the dirty work. We thought we were really something. Never dawned on us we were really suckers. Thinking about it later, I often wondered if maybe the big guys in the Sabers didn't have some other bigger guys telling them what to do. Because we made some pretty good scores. And yet nobody ever had any money. Forty or fifty bucks maybe. That's the most I ever had at any one time.

Not a very illustrious criminal career, any way you look at it. If the kids in Holbrook had known the truth about ole Marshie Jack right from the beginning, things might have been a lot different. Better yet, if Marshie Jack hadn't built it up so much in his own mind. . . .

Anyway, the first time I got caught, nothing happened. A warning and some advice from a judge who obviously didn't believe there was any such thing as a thirteen-year-old professional boy burglar. The second time, I got probation. Third time—about six months later—I got probation again, with stricter supervision. It didn't matter. The way things were going at that time, nothing mattered. Nothing but keeping up with the Sabers, keeping up my front, keeping away from the man. I never went to school, only went home sometimes to sleep and eat.

On my fourth bust the judge sent me to Marshfield. During my first two years my mother used to come for visits once or twice a month. Marshfield was eighty miles from Cleveland, and sometimes she couldn't make the trip. And then, with no warning, I didn't see her or hear from her for a long time. A bad long time. Finally I got a letter from Los Angeles. She had gone out there with some guy—some guy full of promises and God knows what else. And, of course, he had ditched her. She said she had a job as a waitress and she'd be sending me some money and when I got out we'd make a new life and on and on like that.

It was the last time I ever heard from her. What she did was get in touch with Uncle Fred and Aunt Frieda. I had almost forgotten that I even had an uncle Fred and an aunt Frieda. My mother didn't get along with them for some reason, and we never saw them. I don't know what she told them in her letter. When they first came down to Marshfield to see me, they told me she was all right and not to worry. I knew that was baloney. After that they quit talking about her, and I didn't ask. Maybe that sounds hardhearted or something? No. I had already learned the hard way that there are certain things you really can't do anything about, and the only way you can keep going is to put them out of your mind. I still cared about my mother, and I still wanted to see her. . . .

But to get back. When I went to Marshfield, I had never been locked up before, except for a few weeks in a J.D.

center, and was not about to accommodate myself to the place. A boys' school, they called it. Yeah, like San Quentin is a men's school. Marshfield was a reformatory, pure and simple, with locks and guards and a high double fence and a hundred rules. It was run on a system of punishments and rewards. The punishments were usually part of the official policy. The rewards were not. What I mean is you got punished, with anything from missing a movie to ten days in lock-up, whenever you were caught breaking a rule. You might not like the punishments or think they were very fair, but you got used to them after a while, like blisters or rainy weather.

The rewards department, though, was a different proposition, and I never did get used to that one. First of all, there weren't too many rewards available in a place like Marshfield. Late passes, cushy jobs, extra library, stuff like that. True, you might occasionally fall into a good job just by keeping your nose clean, but most of these plums were handed out for ass-kissing the guards and teachers, for being a fink, for conning the administration or the parole board. I guess what you really got rewarded for was learning to play a sneaky game of rotten politics. One thing you did not get rewarded for was trying in your own best way to find out where you were at and how you had gotten there and how you might get to a place you would like better. For example, you could ask for counseling if you wanted it, sure. But if you were really con-wise you wouldn't start doing any yoga or Zen meditation by yourself in the dayroom. Not that that kind of activity was officially frowned on—what it did was label you as some kind of a nut. And the some-kind-of-nut category never led to anything good.

My first two years there, I spent trying to learn to play the con game against the administration, along with another more brutal and complicated game of simple survival in the inmate population. It would take another book to tell that story. Anyway, by the time I was sixteen I had learned to take care of myself pretty well, so I cut loose from most of the gangs and groups and picked up a reputation as a loner. Being a loner in a place like Marshfield is no easy trip, either, but for some people it may be the only way.

I started to do a lot of reading, and that got me to thinking about things that were new to me. I started to get big urges to do something and *be* something. I didn't know exactly what. They had an evening art class, and I joined that and found out I had no talent for drawing. Next I tried to learn to play the guitar and found out I wasn't any good at that either. Maybe I was too impatient and maybe I expected too much of myself. I had this idea that if I couldn't be really good at a thing, I didn't want to bother with it. An attitude that led me finally to concentrate more and more on sports. I didn't think sports were important in the way that real art might be important, but I was good at them; and when I was running loose on the football field I sometimes got so lost in what I was doing that I didn't realize until later how great I had been feeling out there. That getting lost in a thing, forgetting all about myself for a while and in a way becoming the thing I was doing—that was the best feeling in life to me, and up till then sports was the only place I had found it.

And, of course, there was Chuck Grossman. He only had to grin at you a couple of times and you knew he knew. Not that he ever put it that way. He wasn't a philosopher and he wasn't a do-gooder; he was just a straight-ahead sort of guy who seemed to like his job and took a real interest in kids who wanted to learn some of the things he knew how to teach. He taught me how to play football. Nobody else at Marshfield ever taught me much of anything—at least not on purpose.

When I got out of Marshfield and registered at Holbrook High School, I had intended to go out for football and maybe basketball and baseball, too. I wanted to see how I would do against these free-world kids, and I wanted more of that good getting-lost feeling. But then something happened. My first day in school—all those guys and girls who knew each other and always seemed to be moving so fast and sure of themselves, like they had everything all locked up—I just wasn't ready for it. I tried to tell myself that things would be okay after a while, after I got to know some of them, but it didn't work. It was probably the girls more than anything. I wasn't used to girls, especially girls who were as grown-up as these girls. I felt like an outsider and a clunk. And naturally the more I felt like that, the worse it got.

So I decided not to go out for football, after all. The one thing I wanted to do most . . . I decided to pass up. It's incredible what you can let your head do to you sometimes. If Coach Foss hadn't stopped me in the hall that afternoon, I never would have played football; and if I hadn't played football, God knows what the rest of my year would have been like. Of course, something else might have come along to turn me around. You never know when some little thing is going to turn your life around.

But anyway, here it was Friday afternoon, the day before the first game of the season, and I was feeling a lot different and a lot better than I had a week ago. In fact, I was feeling so good that I told Foss I thought I was ready to play.

"Well, you know that's out of the question." The coach frowned at me. "First off, you don't know the timing of the plays. Your head might know them, but your body doesn't—not in relation to the ten other bodies that make those plays work."

"I know."

"And second, and more important yet, your body isn't used to violent physical contact. Best way in the world to

14

get hurt is to go out there and get clotheslined before your body's ready for it.''

"I know. I know. I was just wishin', that's all.''

"We can win this one without you,'' the coach said. "Kirby's the one team on our schedule I know we *can* beat.''

Trouble was, somebody forgot to tell that to Kirby. Because at halftime on that Saturday afternoon, first game of the season, against a team that had lost fifteen straight, proud old Holbrook High was down 8–6.

Coach tore up some egos in the locker room. Went right through the team, player by player. Told most of them they looked like they were trying to impress somebody in the stands instead of trying to win a football game. Spent the last five minutes hammering on that old team-play theme. I'd heard it all before. So had the rest of them. But he was a good talker. He got the spirit going, and when the call came we all went charging out of that locker room like a herd of buffalo who had just smelled green pasture. Even me, though I wasn't going to play that day and didn't really give much of a damn whether we won or lost.

The Kirby team must have heard a good speech, too. They came out snarling like a pack of wolves. They weren't big and they weren't all that fast, but they were organized and they were high on themselves and they were lucky . . . and sometimes luck can make all the difference.

Holbrook played good football that half. Most of the offense was straight-ahead power. The fullback, Kevin Torrance, carried ten out of twelve on one drive. We got to their two . . . third and goal . . . and one of those pesky Kirby wolves came leaping from nowhere, had Torrance by the ankles almost before he got the handoff, and then it was fourth and four. Our placekicker, Teddy Aronson, missed . . . wide, by three inches. And that's the way the game kept going. In the middle of the fourth period Coach Foss called for a time-out. Mostly he let Benny Younger call his own game, but every now and then he'd direct traffic himself for a play or two.

"You guys are going great," he said in the time-out huddle. "But this Kirby team is keying on our ground game. So I want you to start throwing, Benny. We'll go to our two-minute offense right now. Maybe we can surprise 'em. Pass on first down. Either a zig-out to Burt or a flag pattern to Chris, use your own judgment."

So Benny rared back and threw the zig-out. If you don't know, the zig-out is a pattern where the receiver starts downfield, cuts to the outside, then to the inside, and then makes his real cut, back toward the sideline. If there is one pass that shouldn't be intercepted, it's probably the zig-out. But Benny Younger never saw the weak safety, who had fallen down while trying to stay with Chris Buchanan and was now scrambling around hopelessly looking for something to do. By the time Benny released, the safety man was exactly in line with the flight of the ball. It came into his hands like a Christmas present. Benny had to make the touchdown-saving tackle himself on our twelve-yard line.

After three futile plunges over the middle, Kirby called in a wolf cub. The guy couldn't have been over five feet tall, but he kicked a perfect field goal and the score was 11–6, favor of the wolves.

I'd been watching their right linebacker and cornerback all afternoon. They had a weakness that our team hadn't been able to take advantage of. Pumping myself full of whatever confidence I could locate, I left the bench and approached Coach Foss where he was prowling the sidelines.

"Coach, I suppose I'm outa line, but the right side of their defense is pretty slow. I think I could get around them."

He gave me a look. My confidence balloon split a seam.

But then he started to grin. "Look, I don't mind the free advice. And I know you could get around them. But you're not playing today," he said, spacing the words carefully, the way you'd talk to a person who's a little dense. "Now go back and sit down and don't worry about it."

I went back and sat down and kept my red face aimed at the ground for about eight plays, and when I looked up there was 1:26 on the clock and the score was still 11–6.

Holbrook had the ball on the Kirby twenty-two. Benny tried Peanuts Gilliam, the halfback, on a sweep and Gilliam got nailed by the linebacker for no gain. Then Benny passed to Burt Angstrom, standing all alone at the six. Burt made the fatal mistake of trying to run before he got the ball. Incomplete. So, third and still ten to go and only forty-three seconds left in the game. Benny Younger asked the ref for a time-out and came running to the sidelines. No way he was going to call this play on his own.

"Jack! *Delaney!*" I thought I was hearing things, but I grabbed my helmet and raced to where the coach and Benny were standing. "I know I'm wrong. I know I'm crazy," Foss said. And he did look a little crazy, at that. Usually so calm you couldn't surprise him with a cherry bomb. Now wild-eyed and scratching his bald head like he was trying to find a brain.

"Benny, I want you to run Jack on a power sweep to the left. Count of two. And get around fast or this guy'll be past you before you can give him the ball."

"What?" Benny Younger's face had the same expression you see in old Three Stooges comedies.

"You heard me. Now get out there and do what I told you."

"Yes, sir." Benny looked at me. I looked at him. I couldn't help grinning. He didn't grin back.

Nobody welcomed me in the huddle. They looked at me

like I was maybe the water boy or one of the cheerleaders. I didn't blame them. I had never practiced with them, never even talked much to most of them, just said a few words in the locker room. These Holbrook kids, even the guys on the team, were still keeping a cautious distance between themselves and old felonious Jack.

"Twenty-two . . . seventeen. . . . Hut! Hut!" Benny spun with the ball and I had to take short steps, so I wouldn't be past him. I tucked the ball in and headed for the left sideline. The pulling guard was too slow. I couldn't wait for him. My only interference was Torrance. I put my hand on his back, waited till he hit the defensive end. Now I was free. The linebacker who was coming for me had no chance. I head-faked the cornerback and left him with his feet crossed. Nothing between me and the goal line but the free safety. I'd meet him at about the two. He wasn't very big. I knew I could run right through him. He hit me at the three. I ran right through him, into the end zone standing up.

Trouble was . . . the ball didn't go with me. That hyped-up little wolf of a safety man had gone for the ball instead of me. Punched it right out of my arm. I felt it go and couldn't do anything. By the time I got myself stopped and turned around, the safety had fallen on the ball and, with twenty seconds to play, this game was forever down the drain.

"Don't blame it on Jack," Coach Foss was saying in the locker room for about the tenth time. "I should probably be barred from coaching for pulling a stunt like that. Not because we lost the game. To hell with the game. But for taking a chance like that. I could've got him killed!''

"Forget it, coach." Benny Younger said it to him like a father. "You're always telling us not to look back. So . . . nobody's looking back."

Foss gave him a tight smile. "Thanks." Then he beckoned to his assistant and they left the room together.

"That's all fine and dandy," somebody muttered behind me, "but the fact remains this hotshot did lose the game for us."

I turned and looked straight into the eyes of Peanuts Gilliam, the running back I had replaced for that one disastrous play. He was about my height and maybe ten pounds heavier. Watching him play, I'd been thinking he might have made a good lineman. I didn't know him at all. He'd never even said hello to me.

I stared at him for a second. He stared back, eyes hard. "Somethin' bothering you?" he said.

I felt that old red rage coming up inside me, almost like the first days at Marshfield, where a new kid had to either fight or go under—no middle way. But I remembered just in time that this wasn't Marshfield and got hold of myself and said, "No, I guess not," and turned away from him and pulled off my shoulder pads and sat down on a bench.

"Takes more than speed to make a football player," Gilliam said, probably talking to one of his buddies. Maybe talking to me. I sat still and could feel the strain in my shoulders. "Takes some guts," Gilliam said.

Okay. Okay. So it was going to happen anyway. Marshfield or Holbrook, maybe it was all the same. I turned toward him again, swinging my legs over the bench and facing him directly. "If you've got anything to say to me, say it."

His face was innocent. He was one of those long-haired blond guys who look the way most people think athletes are supposed to look.

"I got nothin' to say to you, hotshot." Gilliam stood there, hands at his sides, staring down at me, very cool.

"Don't call me hotshot."

"What do you want me to call you . . . Marshie?"

Guys were starting to look at us. I was sort of hoping one of the coaches would come back in the room, and at the same time hoping he wouldn't.

"Hey, cut it out, Peanuts!" somebody hollered. Sounded like Benny Younger.

"Ain't nothin' happenin'," Peanuts said, drawling it out. "Ole Marshie Jack here's just gonna take himself a nice lukewarm shower and trot on home. Ain't you, Marshie?"

"Peanuts, what the hell is the matter with you!" This from Kevin Torrance, who was standing right beside me.

I stood up and without any warning threw a hard left hook at Peanuts's gut. He blocked it easily. I saw his right fist coming, but couldn't even start to duck. It landed high on my cheekbone. Knocked me completely over the bench. I was flat on my back on the floor. I wasn't hurting. Just crazy mad. So Peanuts was a boxer. I'd tangled with a few boxers before. Knew I couldn't handle a good one straight up. My style, when things got tight, was strictly street fighter.

I got up off the floor, kicked the bench out of the way, and faced Peanuts Gilliam. He was grinning. Very confident.

"Want some more, hotshot?"

There wasn't a sound in the locker room. I moved a half-step toward Peanuts, staring straight in his eyes. And then with the side of my bare foot I kicked him as hard as I could, right on his kneecap. Didn't knock him down, but did knock him off balance. I moved in quick, and this time the left to the gut landed. It was a good punch, caught him exactly in the solar plexus. His breath went—"whoosh!"—and as he doubled over, for the moment almost totally paralyzed, I saw the spot on the back of his neck where the karate chop would do the most good. Or harm.

In the old days, when I was fighting for what I thought was my life, I'd have cut him down any way I could. But now I stepped back, watching Peanuts sag to his knees, gasping desperately for the breath that wouldn't come.

"Hey, we better get him some help!" somebody said.

"He'll be all right," Benny Younger said in a calm voice. "It's just his wind."

I looked around at Benny. He was a tall skinny guy with one of those long, lantern-jawed faces. He gave me a puzzled frown. "I don't know, Jack. I'm not saying I blame you for what you did. Peanuts has had it coming for a long time. But I'll tell you, he's not that bad a guy. And another thing is . . . I guess it's just that we don't fight that way around here."

"Aw, come off it, Benny," Jake Johnson said with a grin. Jake was a black guy, one of the few in Holbrook. He played free safety, and also did most of the kick return work. Since he was probably the fastest man on the team, I had been wondering during the game why the coach didn't use him on offense.

"Far as I'm concerned, that's the only way anybody *can* fight a guy like Peanuts," somebody else said. I looked at him, didn't even know his name, played second-string linebacker. "I'll agree he's not that bad a guy. But standing up and trying to fistfight with Peanuts is just asking to get your damned head knocked off."

"What're you boys doing, holding a pep rally?" It was Coach Foss, back from wherever he'd been. We were all standing in a circle around Peanuts, who was sitting on a bench now, his head still down, fighting for some easy oxygen.

"Listen, put this game away. Maybe you shouldn't forget it, but don't worry about it. Now go out and have yourselves a good time till Monday, because that's when the real work starts. We're going to be ready for Millersville next Saturday, and we're going to beat them. Take the old man's word for it." He gave us a wave and a grin and went out the door.

I stood for a moment, gazing into the empty space where he'd been standing. He was quite a man. Knew how to bounce back. He could admit his mistakes, feel real lousy for a while, and then put them behind him and go on. To the next game or the next day or the next minute. That's the way I wanted to be.

"Listen, Delaney." It was Peanuts, sitting on his bench, looking up at me. "I'm gonna let you win this round, for a couple of reasons. But you stay outa my way from now on. Because you won't walk away from the next round. You understand?"

I stared into his eyes for a second, trying to find the balancing point of this situation, and decided we were on it. We could both let it go now, for a while anyway. Actually, what I was thinking was that I might just dump this whole football scene. Not because of Peanuts—and not because of the fumble, but because I had a strong feeling that being on this team would just lead to one complication after another. I wanted to play, sure I did, but I didn't want this kind of trouble.

Maybe I should take up chess or some other lonesome game, I was thinking, as I took off my supporter and got in the shower. There were thirty or so other guys in the long steamy shower stall, and I felt like I was all alone, maybe in Japan or somewhere. Nobody spoke to me. I didn't even look at anybody.

While I was toweling off, though, Benny Younger came up. "Hey, Jack. What're you doing tonight?"

I shrugged. "Nothing, I guess."

"Well, listen. There's a party at Linda Gerhardt's house. She's my girl friend. Why don't you come along? I know where your uncle lives. I'll pick you up about eight.''

"Oh . . . well, thanks, but I don't think so.''

"Why not? It's time to get out and meet some people.'' He gave me a punch on the arm. "You're going to be the star of this football team, man. You don't want all the kids going around saying, 'Jack Who?' "

I couldn't help laughing. Benny had a way about him. Probably end up making a million dollars selling life insurance.

"Well, I don't have a girl friend, Benny. And I've never been one for parties. Honest to God, I wouldn't know what to do.'' Which kind of surprised me. It wasn't my style to go around admitting things like that.

"You don't need a girl friend. It's not that kind of a party. You don't have to do anything. Just bring your body. Good things will happen. I guarantee it!''

So I surprised myself again and said okay. And I went to the party. But first I had to go through a little bit of a hard time with my uncle Fred.

"Heard you had some bad luck today.'' Uncle Fred had a habit of bringing up serious subjects at the supper table. "Course, I didn't see it myself. You know you told us you wouldn't be playing today.''

I glanced at Aunt Frieda. She was carefully inspecting her fried chicken.

"I blew the game. Coach gave me a shot and I blew the game. It wasn't bad luck. It was just stupidity.''

"Now, don't be so hard on yourself. Corwin Williams

saw the game, and he told me Holbrook couldn't have won anyway without that run you made. Wait'll next week. You'll prob'ly get another chance."

"I don't know. I think I might give it up."

"Now why do you want to act like that? Corwin said you looked real good out there till you fumbled." Uncle Fred gnawed on a chicken leg for a few minutes. Then he wiped his mouth with his napkin and gave me a sudden fierce look. "You remind me a lot of your daddy, Jack. I mean the way you're acting right now. He had all the talent in the world, coulda been almost anything he set his mind to. But as soon as something went wrong, he'd quit. Just say to hell with it and go off and try something else.

"Now don't get me wrong," he added. "In a lot of ways your daddy—who happened to be my brother, don't forget that! In a lot of ways he was the finest man you could find in a month of Sundays, and the smartest, too. But he had this thing in him that said he had to be the best at anything he did. Which is not a bad thing in itself, believe me. But your daddy wouldn't work *hard* at anything. He believed in natural talent. He believed you could either do a thing or you couldn't do it. And if you couldn't do it, first crack out of the box, then to hell with it."

My uncle shook his head. "I don't have to tell you what he finally decided were his best natural talents. Drinkin' and general hell-raisin'. And at thirty-two he was dead, head split wide open by a pool cue, killed by an ignorant violent bastard, who on his best days wasn't fit to carry your daddy's shoes on your daddy's worst days."

"Fred, I don't see anything to be gained by going through all that old stuff again," Aunt Frieda said sharply.

"Maybe not." Uncle Fred glanced at me. "I'm not trying to torment you, boy. You know that. I just want . . . I just hope you won't quit because you made one mistake or got one bad break."

One mistake. One bad break. I knew that's how it must look to my uncle. And I knew I couldn't explain to him what all the ins and outs really were.

I also knew and knew and knew all about my dad. I could even remember him pretty well. Big, strong, graceful as a leopard, even when he was drunk out of his mind. He never got falling-down drunk, never got stupid and slurry. What liquor did to him was something inside, something in his head. What liquor did to him was make him crazy. Like, he was a good pool-shooter. Best in our neighborhood. He could win ten or twenty dollars a night shooting eight-ball down at Barney's, which was a neighborhood bar with two pool tables in it.

My dad was no hustler. Everybody in the neighborhood knew him, and a lot of guys were willing to lose a buck or two just for the fun of playing against him. Because when my dad was sober, or even only halfway sober, he was just about the best guy you'd ever want to meet to play any kind of game with.

But then he'd get drunk and he'd get this idea he was not only the best in the neighborhood, he was the best in the city. So he'd go down to Paramount Billiards, where the really best shooters in the city, plus hustlers from all over the state, hung out; and he'd play nine-ball for ten dollars a ball. And he'd blow a hundred, two hundred, maybe more, depending on how much money he had.

Uncle Fred thought he was a quitter. But in some things my dad was just the opposite. Especially when he was drunk. His motto seemed to be: Never quit till you're broke . . . or dead. Trouble was, he used that motto for all the wrong things. Always trying to beat the other guy at the other guy's own game. Maybe my dad was a certain kind of born loser, I don't know. What I do know is he wasn't any kind of easy quitter.

What I really think—and my mother told me once she

thought so, too—is that my dad had a kind of huge sadness in him. For some reason, and nobody ever found out why, he just couldn't seem to live with himself sober for more than two or three weeks at a time. And it was so senseless, so tragic. Because my dad, sober, was one hell of a guy. Everybody who ever knew him said the same thing. The only person who never believed it was my dad himself.

My mother was a different kind of person. She didn't drink and she seldom got very mad about anything, or very enthusiastic either. I guess she was kind of a drifter in a way—making the best of whatever was there, not worrying about things that were out of reach. That was fine as long as my dad was around, because even with his drinking and gambling, he always seemed to pay the rent first and keep food on the table. Or maybe he didn't always pay the rent first. I was only seven when he died, and I probably didn't even know what rent was. But I know that I never went hungry, and I remember that our house was a happy place when my dad was alive.

After he died, things changed pretty fast. We had to move to a small apartment on the fourth floor of a crummy building, my mother and me, and we lived there alone except for once in a while, when my mother's sister would come to visit for a few days. That was in the beginning. Later things changed again. My mother started getting tangled up with different guys. I wasn't old enough to understand then. It made me feel sick and lousy, and I started cutting school and staying away from home as much as I could. I realize now that my mother couldn't help it. She just wasn't built to live alone, and the too-bad thing was that she never had any luck. Every guy she met turned out to be a loser. Drunks, junkies, tired pilgrims looking for a short rest—they could spot her a mile away. I never figured out how or why. My mother was a good-looking woman, and she kept herself up. She didn't look like any kind of a slob or pushover. But there was something about her . . . like she wore a sign that said soft touch. After my dad died, my mother never had a chance. I don't know, maybe she didn't want a chance.

"You must have got hit pretty good," my uncle Fred said, bringing me back to the present.

"Why?"

"Well, that bruise under your eye. It's cut, too. Looks like somebody belted you."

"It *is* a nasty bruise, Jack." Aunt Frieda was peering at me in some alarm. "I don't know why I never noticed. Do you get hurt like that every time you play football?"

"Nah. Anyway, it's just a little bruise." You oughta see what *can* happen to you when you play football—that's what I was thinking, but, of course, I wasn't going to tell her.

"Hey, is it okay if I go out tonight?"

"Why, of course, it's okay!" Aunt Frieda gave me one of her happy, but always slightly tremulous, smiles. "It's about time you started going out and having some fun for yourself."

"Got yourself a galfriend?" Uncle Fred winked a sly man-to-man wink.

"Nah. It's some kind of a party. Benny Younger invited me. Said I didn't need a girl friend."

"They'll probably play whist or bingo or somethin'," Uncle Fred said solemnly. "I hear that's what the kids are up to these days."

I had to grin. Uncle Fred could get under my skin sometimes, but he was a sharp old dude just the same.

The party turned out to be . . . what? I don't know. I'd never been to a party like that before. In fact, I'd never been to any real parties at all. Just the wild bashes we used to have in the Sabers' clubhouse when I was on the street before I got sent to Marshfield. I was only thirteen, doing a few burglaries, smoking a little dope, and trying to make out with the girls. Maybe that's part of the reason why it was hard for me to talk to girls now that I was eighteen. The kind of girls who came to our clubhouse never had time to fool around with some thirteen-year-old punk kid. And then, of course, at Marshfield there weren't any girls at all. One thing I never did do when I was in the gang was drink. Maybe because I had seen what booze did to my dad. But by the time I was fourteen I had tried just about everything else that was available—and none of it had prepared me for this party at Benny Younger's girl's house.

A few of the kids were drinking beer, but nobody got drunk. Nobody was smoking grass, at least not that I could see or smell. Nobody got in a fight. Nobody even got in a hassle about whose girl was whose . . . or vice versa. Benny introduced me around. I knew most of the kids by sight, from school. And I did notice a few guys from the team there. Everybody was friendly enough. They'd say, "Hi, Jack. Nice to see you," or something like that, and then kind of drift away or get in a conversation with someone else.

After a while I found myself standing off to one side, drinking a Pepsi and trying to figure out what the hell kind of a party this was supposed to be. And also feeling pretty much out of it. Whatever *it* was. Because it seemed to me that nobody was doing anything. Nothing was happening. The stereo was on, but soft, not blasting the way I always used to listen to music. And the records were mostly folk and country rock. Not the kind of music I'd ever listened to very much.

Well, this is Holbrook, I told myself. Holbrook ain't Cleveland. Get that through your thick head. But then I realized that didn't make too much sense, either. Because I'd heard the eight-tracks blasting in some of the cars in the school parking lot and it was the same hard rock and disco stuff you'd hear in Cleveland or Marshfield or New York City, for that matter.

28

Actually, what you're doing, I said to myself, is feeling sorry for yourself again. What you really want is for these people to come crowding around you, saying they love you just because you're you.

"Oh, Jack . . . ?"

I looked up. It was Linda Gerhardt, with another girl, a stranger.

"This is Cindy Farr," Linda said. "Jack Delaney."

I took a step forward to shake hands, and almost fell down.

"Cindy's my cousin," Linda said, politely ignoring my tremendous poise. "She's up from Columbus for the weekend." Then she walked away, leaving me staring stupidly at the prettiest girl I had ever seen in my life. But "pretty" isn't exactly the right word. Cindy Farr was more than pretty . . . and maybe less than pretty. She had shiny black hair, parted in the middle, falling soft and loose to just below her shoulders. She had huge dark-brown eyes that looked at you wide open, with no tricks and no fear. And the funny thing was, she had kind of a big nose, a strong high-arched nose that fit her face just right. Her face, and her look, sort of stunned me. All I could do for a minute was stare back at her.

"I saw you play this afternoon," she said. "Why didn't the coach put you in sooner?"

"I wasn't ready. I mean I came out for the team late."

She was gazing into my eyes, not probing, but looking deep, as though interested in whatever she saw there. I could feel heat coming up in my face. And I noticed how tall she was . . . maybe five-eight or -nine. I wanted to look away . . . but I didn't want to look away, either. And it didn't matter what I wanted, because it felt as though somebody else had control of my eyes and there was no way in God's world I could look away from her.

"My brothers play football," she said, finally taking her eyes from mine. "Do you want to sit down?"

"Uh . . . yeah. You sit in the chair. I'll sit on the floor."

"Let's both sit on the floor."

So we both sat on the floor, cross-legged, facing each other, in front of the empty chair. Usually I don't notice clothes, but I noticed hers. Dark-brown corduroy jacket, light-brown corduroy pants, soft leather boots with zippers on the sides. Nothing flashy, nothing grubby, everything just right.

"I'm no expert on football," she said. "But I watch my brothers. And my dad's a football maniac. I think you're probably a good player."

She had a button pinned to the lapel of her jacket. A white plastic button with a picture of a whale on it.

"What's the whale stand for?"

"I'm in a movement that's trying to save the whales. Some of them are almost extinct, you know. And if we can't get the Russians and the Japanese to stop hunting them, there just won't be any whales left in a few years."

"Is that right?" I had practically no interest in whales, or hadn't up until that minute. But all of a sudden they seemed like a good subject for conversation, so I started asking dumb questions, and she told me a whole lot of stuff about whales and dolphins and the big trouble they were in. It seemed a littly nutty—sitting here in this warm house in Ohio, a thousand miles from an ocean, talking about a bunch of whales neither one of us had ever seen. But then I'd catch the sincerity and concern in her voice, and it wouldn't seem nutty at all. Maybe the whales did need somebody out in Ohio to worry about them . . . and then I sort of flashed on something else: Maybe it wasn't a one-way street. Maybe Cindy Farr needed the whales, too. Anyway, whatever it was, it was real and it was good; and though I had started the conversation just to have something to talk about, I found I was getting indignant about the whole rotten whale-murdering business.

"You can't be all that interested in whales," she said with a slow smile that spread from her mouth to her cheeks to her eyes and eyebrows . . . man! She didn't smile as much as some, but when she did, the smile just seemed to come up from inside her and take over everything. "My brothers think I'm crazy." She pressed her lips together and made a face that was funny and sweet and sad and amazing. "Let's talk about football."

"Football's no fun to talk about. It's fun to play, but boring to talk about."

"You ought to tell that to my dad." She laughed. And her expression went through some other changes. She'd tighten her lips to try to stop smiling, but the smile would keep bursting through, quick and quirky, here and gone.

I was looking at her, trying to keep up with her, wishing I was good at telling stories or making jokes . . . getting that knotted-up feeling that leads to nothing but more knots.

"Uh . . . do you go to school in Columbus?"

She nodded, made another face, and waved her hand. It was the best answer about school that anybody could give, but of course old dumbhead Jack had to keep pushing along because he didn't know what else to do.

"What school do you go to?"

"Columbus School for Girls." She smiled kind of a tight smile, and her eyes were suddenly narrow and challenging. "Isn't that awful?"

I felt about six inches tall. She was probably on a weekend furlough. She didn't look it . . . but what kind of baloney was that! Nobody looked it. There were a hundred things I wanted to say to her . . . and I couldn't think of one.

"Well, I think I'll get a sandwich." And she was on her feet and gone before I could get my legs uncrossed. By the time I caught up with her, she was talking to two other guys out in the kitchen. I took a chicken-salad sandwich from a tray on the counter and stood around for a minute, trying to get my nerve up to join her . . . or hoping she'd look at me and leave the other guys and come over and talk to me again. No good. She thought I'd put her down about being in that school for girls. And I sure as hell couldn't blame her. But for me to do it, of all people. Trouble was, she didn't know I was "of all people." And even if she did, it would probably only make matters worse. She might even have a clause in her furlough papers saying she shouldn't associate with anybody who'd been in a reformatory.

I didn't know what to do, so I went back in the living room and tried to eat my sandwich. Everybody seemed to be talking to somebody else. I knew I was being stupid, but knowing it didn't help very much. It seemed impossible for me to go up and talk to anybody, or to stand around pretending to enjoy myself.

Next thing I knew I was outside, walking, then running. Toward or away from . . . I didn't know. I was just running . . . down dark quiet streets . . . September night cool and lonesome against my face.

"Hey, what happened to you Saturday night?" Benny Younger caught up to me in the hall. It was Monday. I was on my way to homeroom, keeping my eyes straight ahead, sort of waiting for somebody to make a crack about the fumble. "Everybody at the party was wondering where you went," Benny said. "Specially Cindy Farr."

"Yeah, I bet."

"Maybe you got bored. Our parties are kind of quiet, I guess. Till you get used to them." I could see Benny looking at me. I shot him a sideways glance. He didn't seem to be ribbing me. "We're not squares," Benny said. "We're just interested in different things than . . . oh, say, Peanuts and his crowd."

"Yeah? What're Peanuts and his crowd interested in?"

"You know. Booze, decibels, driving ninety miles an hour . . . smoking dope when they can get it . . . cheap sex. . . ."

"Why, that sounds just terrible!"

Benny flushed. "Come on, Jack! We don't put all those things down all the time. We just like to try for something else."

"I know. Listen, you guys are all right. It was a good party. Sometimes I just have to act like a creep . . . I don't know why."

"Aaah . . . that's okay." Benny grinned. "See you at practice this after."

I wanted to tell him I wasn't going to be there, but decided I couldn't act like a creep twice in two minutes.

I went into my homeroom and sat down and thought about Cindy Farr. Yeah. I bet she was wondering where I went. She probably asked Benny, "What happened to that creep who was talking to me?"

"How are you doin', Delaney?" It was Jake Johnson, who sat across from me. We'd never had much to say to each other, which was no doubt as much my fault as his. I told him I was doing okay and he said, "See you at practice," and I said okay before I thought.

I glanced at Jake Johnson. He was deep in a paperback. I wondered how it felt to be a black guy in a school like Holbrook. I knew that there wasn't the kind of tension between blacks and whites here that you'd find in some of the city schools and in Marshfield. But just because there weren't obvious pressures didn't mean everything was smooth, either. I was pretty sure Jake couldn't go out with a white girl in Holbrook . . . not without both of them running into a whole *lot* of heavy pressure. I didn't know if that was important to Jake. I figured, though, that the principle probably was important. In some ways he and I were in the same boat, always just on the edge of the mainstream, no matter what we did, and no matter how many people told us it wasn't so.

When the bell rang I headed for my first-period class, algebra. One good thing I had already learned about algebra: the teacher was always Mr. Foss, never Coach Foss. Keeping things separate like that can help sometimes.

Holbrook High was one of those sprawly new schools, which meant there could be quite a walk between classes. My homeroom and Mr. Foss's room were at opposite ends of the school. I'd just gotten started when somebody touched my arm and said, "Hi!" It was Lori Curtin, one of the few girls in the school I knew by name . . . and by reputation. Lori was what my uncle Fred would have called a hot number. Which is not to say anything against her, just that she did what she wanted to do and didn't seem to give a damn who liked it or who didn't like it.

"Somebody told me you were going to be our next big football hero." She was pretty . . . blond and blue-eyed . . . with a curve to her lips and a light in her eye that made me feel sort of unusual. "But then somebody else told me you weren't going to be, so I was wondering what you thought."

"Uh. . . ." There I went again, stalling before my motor got revved up. "No hero." I glanced down at her. She was about five-feet-three, and—as my uncle Fred might say—stacked.

She laughed and said she didn't like football anyway, just some of the players. I didn't know what to say, so I laughed, too. It was some conversation. All the way to algebra, she doing most of the talking, and I was throwing in a few uh's and is that right's. Somewhere along the way we passed Peanuts Gilliam, who ignored me but glared at her.

"He thinks I'm his girl," she said, "just because I go out with him. Some boys are so *possessive*." She shot me another one of her slanty glances. "I'll bet you're not the possessive type, are you?"

"Uh. . . ."

"I can't stand boys who think they *own* a person."

"Is that right?"

We reached the door to Mr. Foss's room. "I've got English!" she cried, like it was something really nice. "See you later." Stumbling to my seat in algebra, I remembered that English was back up the hall about half a mile.

The rest of the day went along okay, which meant it wasn't too bad and wasn't too good. I just couldn't seem to get into school the way some people could. Besides algebra, I was taking world history and English and a funny kind of science course that was supposed to be an introduction to physics or chemistry or biology or whatever you might want to take up afterward. All in all, it was the best class I had. I wouldn't say I'd learned a whole lot in those first few weeks, but I was getting little tastes of what science might be about, and some of the tastes were pretty good. Maybe because the teacher was pretty good.

Her name was Mrs. Swanson, and she was around forty and not by any means what you could call a good-looking woman. Short and dumpy, sloppy dresser, hair always wisping out from the little bun she wore on top of her head. But she was in love with science, and she had a way of getting you to see why she was in love with it. My other teachers were . . . I don't know . . . I guess, average. They didn't impress me, and vice versa.

You could say that the courses I was taking didn't seem to add up to much, that they sounded more like ninth grade than twelfth. The reason for that was that before I left Marshfield, Chuck Grossman sat down with me one day and showed me where I was weak, just in case I might want to go to college later. At the time college seemed to be almost impossible, but when I got to Holbrook I signed up for math and science, just in case.

Funny how things work. . . . If I hadn't taken algebra, I might never have gone out for football . . . and if I hadn't gone out for football, I'd never have tangled with Peanuts Gilliam . . . and I'd almost certainly never have met Cindy Farr. So it all started from a football coach in a reformatory suggesting to me one day that I was weak in math and science. But, of course, it didn't start from that, either. Because no matter what point you look back at as a turning point, you can always look farther back and find another turning point.

Anyway, the street I had chosen had led me back to the football field, and when I got to practice that afternoon I wished I had run up some blind alley instead. First thing that happened, even before we got out of the locker room, was that Coach Foss called a meeting for the whole squad. Turned out he had a brand-new assistant coach, young guy named Calvin Pleasance, who wasn't even connected with the school. Foss still had Mel Eakins as his regular assistant, but it seems this guy Pleasance, who had just moved to Holbrook to work in or maybe run his father's drugstore, was a former halfback at Bowling Green and had volunteered to help out as backfield coach if Foss could use him.

That part was all right. The bombshell came after Pleasance had made his little hello speech and we were all scuffing our cleats and waiting to get outside.

"We're going to be making a few changes," Foss said, standing up in front of us again. All the cleat scuffing stopped. "Maybe I've grown too conservative," he went on, shifting his gaze from player to player. "Playing it safe, though, is what it really amounts to. Anyway, from this day on, things are going to be different. With Calvin here we've got a backfield coach who understands the open game, so we're going to give it a shot, and we're going to have us some fun . . . and, by George, we're going to win us some ball games!"

By George! You might have to travel a far piece to find another coach who'd give you a "by George!" But that was just the warm-up. The real news came when we hit the practice field. The starting backfield, for this week anyway, Foss said, would be Benny Younger, Kevin Torrance, Jake Johnson, and Jack Delaney.

"We'll be using wide receivers a lot," Foss said, by way of explanation. "And we've got to have speed. Peanuts, I want to try you on the defense, at linebacker or end, and also use you some of the time in the offensive backfield. Think you could go both ways?"

Peanuts nodded bleakly. It had happened too fast for him really to get hold of it yet.

"And how about you, Jake?" Foss went on. "You've got the speed to be a flanker, and I know you've got good hands. Point is, you're also the best we've got at free safety. Think you can handle both jobs?"

"I'll sure give it a try," Jake said. Then added innocently, "Maybe me and Jack could take turns."

"At flanker? You mean at safety?" Foss looked slightly bug-eyed. "You ever play any defense?" he said to me.

"Some."

"Well, we'll see. But for now, one thing at a time. You concentrate on learning that flanker position, Jake, and let me handle the coaching for another week or two."

It was the kind of thing that could never happen at a bigger school, where there was plenty of talent for two teams or maybe three or four teams. At Holbrook, though, there were only about thirty guys who even came out for football. Coach Foss didn't believe in cutting anybody who wanted to play, and I guess he had always stuck to his two-platoon system because he knew he couldn't field a winning team, anyway, and figured he might as well give his whole squad a chance at losing, instead of just letting the best fifteen or so get their brains knocked out every Saturday.

But now, like he said, things were changing. The new backfield coach had ideas on how to get the best out of what was available. Nothing fancy that first week . . . mostly Jake on a fly or curl, the tight end over the middle, Chris Buchanan down the other sideline, and me going out of the backfield once in a while, usually as a secondary receiver on a flare, or staying in the flat for a simple screen.

Jake took to flanker back like he was born with it. Natural moves and great acceleration. He and Benny looked like they could score five touchdowns a game. Until Pleasance put them up against our defense. And then it was the same old story. Benny Younger didn't seem to have the ability or knack or whatever it takes to scan the field and spot the open man. He could throw receptions nine out of ten, but half of them would be caught by the defense.

"Don't worry about it," Pleasance said to a disheartened Benny. "It'll come to you. We'll keep working at it. Most of it's timing, anyway. And you just haven't had enough practice at it."

So then he tried our second-string quarterback, a junior named Milhalchick. Hopeless. Fine ball handler, good runner, couldn't hit an elephant at twenty yards with a forward pass.

"No problem," Pleasance said. "We won't be passing a whole hell of a lot for a while. But we'll keep running our patterns just the same. Jake'll keep two of their backs busy every time he goes down the field."

"I do believe Millersville is in for a little surprise,"

Coach Foss said after Friday's practice. He was grinning like a kid with a fifty-dollar gift certificate for McDonald's. A lot of coaches would have kept horning in, showing their authority, trying to take credit, and so on. Foss didn't have to do any of that. He was still the boss, and we all knew it. He just sat back and let the offense get as good as it could.

One thing he did do was give Peanuts a try at tight end. I couldn't figure why. He already had a very good tight end in Burt Angstrom. Not that it mattered, because Peanuts turned out to be a lousy catcher. Footballs bounced off him like he was made of wood. He was a bear on defense, though. When we scrimmaged on Thursday, he hit me so hard it rattled my spine. It was the only time I saw him smile all week. Off the field he ignored me, which was all right with me. Maybe we could work it out later. Or maybe not; it didn't seem important.

Not much else happened that week, except when Lori Curtin met me in the hall again and asked me if I was going to the dance at the youth center Saturday night.

"Uh . . . no, I guess not."

"You're a funny guy," she said, giving me one of those slanty looks of hers. "Don't you like girls?"

"Sure I like girls, but I don't know how to dance. That's all."

"Oh, for God's sake! You don't have to know how to dance. Practically nobody knows how to dance anymore. And I know because I *take* dance. All you have to do is get out there and shake that thing a little bit."

I could feel my face getting red. Holbrook a hick school? I got more embarrassed just thinking about how embarrassed I was.

She cut away, into her English class. She sure had a nice walk . . . probably from taking all those dancing lessons.

Then on Friday after practice, Jake Johnson said to me, "Are you comin' to the dance tomorrow night?"

"Aaah, I don't know. To tell you the truth, Jake, I don't know how to dance worth a damn."

"Forget it, man." He laughed. "Ain't no room to dance, anyway. Mostly just an excuse for a little snugglin' and bugglin' with people you ain't never snuggled and buggled before."

"What d'ya mean, 'buggled'?"

"You s'posed to be the big-city hipster," he said, grinning. "How come you're so dumb about certain things?" I just stood there looking at him. Jake was a puzzle. Sometimes he talked like a street-wise city black, and other times he sounded like a college professor.

"You're all right, Jack. Come to the dance, man, and give the ladies a treat."

"Well, maybe. But listen, Jake. You played against Millersville last year. What kinda team they got? Think we can beat 'em?"

"Sure we can. We got a hellaceous team right now. We oughta beat everybody on the schedule 'cept Columbus-Murdock and maybe Townsend."

"What's Columbus-Murdock?"

"Big tech school in Columbus. Only reason they keep scheduling us must be to give their third team a workout. Last year they beat us fifty-two to six."

"Well, maybe we can score a few more points this year."

"Tell it, baby!" Then Jake got serious. "Listen, man . . . I may be wrong about this, but I'm gonna give you a tip just the same, and if I'm wrong we can forget it. Okay?"

"Sure."

"Don't be too surprised if things don't go quite the same tomorrow as they've been going in practice."

"I wouldn't expect them to."

"That's not what I mean. Now, you might not believe this—and like I said it might not happen—but Peanuts

40

Gilliam's got a couple of good buddies in the offensive line, and I won't be too surprised if they miss a block now and then when you're carrying the ball."

"Come on!"

"No jive. And that doesn't mean Peanuts will be telling them to. I *know* they'd be missin' blocks if I was carryin' the ball."

I couldn't believe it. Even at Marshfield, where there were always some heavy feuds going on, nobody ever pulled that kind of stuff in a real game.

"Is that why Foss never played you in the backfield before?"

"More or less."

"Hey, that's lousy! I never thought he'd be that kind of a guy."

Jake shook his head. "He's not. But you gotta understand this town. It's a very tight little town, and uptight, too, in some ways."

"I don't know. It sounds crazy. Was it because you're black?"

"Uh-uh. And that's the part you've got to understand. You see, I lived in Detroit till I was twelve, and I know all about being black. I mean *all* about it. Between me and Peanuts, right from the beginning, black never had anything to do with it."

"I still don't get the picture. Who the hell is Peanuts Gilliam? Does he own the school or something?"

"No, but his old man owns half the town. Peanuts got a brand-new Audi for his sixteenth birthday. Could have had a Maserati if he wanted it. He's a rich kid and he's a *tough* rich kid, and that's a weighty combination, in this town anyway." Jake stopped, frowned, rubbed his jaw. "Funny thing is I used to get the feeling sometimes that Peanuts didn't really want all that power. It was sort of dropped on him . . . but I guess he's gotten used to it."

"Yeah, but what bothers me is, why is Foss willing to

take a chance on a civil war now when he wasn't a couple of years ago?"

"Beats me. Maybe he finally got tired of losing."

"How do you feel about it?"

"I feel okay." Jake grinned. "I didn't want all that weight when I was a freshman, but now that the weight's spread around a little, . . . Yeah, I'd like to see how it feels to play on a winner once."

I was thinking about the whole crazy story while I showered. And I still couldn't get it through my head why Foss, after playing it safe all these years, would suddenly decide to move in exactly the opposite direction. No doubt he was tired of losing, but he must have gotten tired of that a long time ago.

"Hey, Jack!" somebody hollered right in my ear. It was Benny Younger, hair plastered flat to his head from the shower, long bony face twisted in a question mark. "Have you gone deaf or were you in a trance?"

We both stepped out of the shower and grabbed our towels. "I was asking you if you're coming to the dance tomorrow," Benny said.

"Oh, man, I don't know. That must be some kind of a big-deal dance, huh?"

"No. They have them every month at the youth center. Reason I asked was, Cindy Farr's coming up to Linda's for the weekend again. Linda told her we were going to the dance, and Cindy asked about you and wondered whether you were going to be there."

"Are you kidding me?"

Benny had a grin on his face. "I don't know what you've got, Jack, my boy, but you're the first guy in this town that Cindy Farr has ever mentioned."

"She come up here a lot?"

"Yeah, quite a bit." He stopped, and frowned. "I never thought about it before, but I guess there must be something about Columbus she doesn't like too much."

"Look . . . does she know . . . I mean does she know I was in Marshfield?"

"I don't know. I doubt it. Maybe Linda told her, but I doubt it."

I was putting my pants on, buttoning my shirt. After a minute or so, Benny said, "Jack, I don't know how to say this, but that Marshfield thing . . . well, we don't care about that. It doesn't make any difference."

"It doesn't?"

"Not to anybody that's worth a damn. Let me put it that way. It won't make any difference to Cindy Farr, I'll tell you that."

He was very serious. A good, serious guy. "Okay." I pulled my sweater over my head. "I appreciate it."

Later I thought about it and wondered if Benny knew about Cindy and that school for girls. Maybe he didn't, because I wouldn't have known if I hadn't practically forced it out of her.

Cindy Farr. Asking about me? I had kept myself from thinking about her most of the week. But now her image came flooding back. Those eyes, and the sudden unexpected way she smiled. Her concern for whales . . . her shyness. . . . I realized it now: Those swift changes she went through were part of a shyness that didn't seem like shyness . . . and of an openness that wasn't like anything I had ever seen before.

I knew right then I was going to that dance. Maybe I could fake a sprained ankle or something, so I wouldn't have to get out on the floor.

But first there was a football game to be played. My first game for Holbrook. And, as it turned out, the weirdest game I ever played in my life.

We traveled to Millersville in a school bus. It was only about thirty miles, but since I'd never made a trip with a football team, it was an event for me. Most of the guys were joking around and raising a mild kind of hell. They seemed to have accepted me by now—well, maybe not Peanuts and some of his buddies—but, all in all, I was losing the feeling of being old Marshie Jack, the messed-up kid from the reformatory. I did, however, have a strong feeling about going to another team's home field and playing a game in a place I had never seen.

The feeling lasted all through the trip, got stronger while we were sitting around in what looked to be the girls' locker room at Millersville, and then fell away the minute we stepped onto the field. I found that one football field was practically the same as another. The people in the stands and the physical surroundings didn't matter all that much. What mattered were those white lines and the green spaces between them.

Millersville won the toss and decided, for reasons of their own, to kick off. Jake Johnson brought it back to our thirty-six. We went into our huddle, Benny called for the power sweep left, with me carrying the ball. On the first play from scrimmage, I went sixty-four yards for a touchdown.

Now I know that sounds like too much, and maybe even like bragging. But it's not. It's just the way it happened. Everybody got his man. Chris Buchanan threw a sweet block that let me turn the corner, Torrance knocked down a linebacker, Jake got the cornerback, and all I had to do was run away from a couple of guys. Teddy Aronson kicked the extra point; 7–0 in our favor, with the game less than a minute old. A start like that can sometimes blow the other team completely off the field.

Sometimes. Not this time. On their first possession, Millersville held the ball for six minutes, finally punching it over from the three. They were big and confident and methodical. Our defense couldn't hold them. Their quarterback threw only one, almost disdainful, pass, a little flare that was good for eight yards. After they scored, instead of going for the tie, they sent their fullback through the middle for an easy two points.

Jake got the kickoff again and was smothered before he hit the twenty. As we trotted onto the field, Benny Younger said, "This might turn out to be a long afternoon. I think we need at least four touchdowns."

"Maybe more like six. Our defense is going to get tired quicker than their offense."

He scowled and said, "Yeah" . . . and called a pass play, a long bomb to Jake. I winced, both from fear of an interception and because I was thinking our best bet might be to try to hold onto the ball ourselves for a while and give our defense a rest.

My assignment on that play was to follow Jake down for ten yards and then break over the middle. When I finished my route, I saw Benny heave the ball with everything he had; and downfield I saw that Jake had a step on the deep man. Looked good. But then I saw the ball sail so far over Jake's head that he couldn't have reached it with a stepladder.

Back in the huddle Benny said, "Sorry, Jake, but that was mainly to put some fear in the bastards. Keep 'em from keying on Jack and Kevin. We know you can beat that guy now. Slow down a step or two till he gets brave again, and then we'll zonk him."

Next play was Torrance carrying on a slant over tackle. He got four tough yards, mostly on his own. The Millersville defense was digging in. Third and six, and maybe it hadn't been so smart to waste that down after all. Benny called for the halfback draw. It's a nice little piece of deception. Quarterback fades as though to pass. Certain defenders are allowed to penetrate. Then quarterback hands off to halfback, who zips through the open middle for a long gainer—you hope. This time, though, there was no hope. I was met at the line by a guard who was supposed to have been brush-blocked to the outside. Well, it happens. All you can do is pick yourself up and hope you get the ball back before the opposition scores.

Which we did, by recovering a fumble on their forty. First play in the new series was power sweep right, with me carrying. My interference broke down and I got only two yards. Torrance picked up three and then Benny called for the screen. Looked to me like a good call. They were rushing us hard, and the screen was the perfect way to beat that kind of aggressive defense.

Benny dropped back, pumped a couple of times as though to throw downfield, then dumped the ball off to me on the right flank. It was thrown perfectly. I tucked it in, pivoted, looking for my blockers, and saw only two big green Millersville jerseys. I did manage to get back to the line of scrimmage, but it was an awful lot of work for a no-gain play. So now it was fourth and five on their thirty-five. Too long for a field goal, too short for a punt, unless you've got a guy who can drop them in the corners, and our punter, Mike Angelli, was a boomer, not a pinpoint bomber.

"These guys are waiting for me," I said, back in the huddle. "Maybe we oughta fake to me and let Torrance do the carryin'."

"You musta really scared 'em with that touchdown," Wally Koninsberg said. Wally was our left tackle . . . big, slow, not too smart, but a blocker you could count on when you needed a hole. I stared at him. Was he trying to be a wiseass? I didn't know him very well, but he hadn't struck me that way.

"Okay, cool it!" Benny said. He glanced at me, obviously puzzled. I didn't blame him. He'd been counting on me. They all had. I was supposed to be the flash who was going to turn the running game around; and except for that lucky touchdown, I'd picked up a total of two yards in three carries, which could happen to anybody. Granted. What was probably bothering Benny was my copping out as soon as the going got a little rough. What was bothering me was something else. I didn't really want to recognize it, but I knew what it was, all right.

"Look, I'll carry the ball," I said. "Anything you say."

"We're out of time," Benny said, lips tight. "Red sixty-six. Flag, on three." It was the fly pattern to Jake, turning to the outside. On this one I had to help protect the quarterback, and Millersville's blitzing safety kept me so busy I never saw the play develop. But a groan from the stands told me something good must have happened for our side. When I got untangled from the safety man, I saw Jake standing in the end zone holding the ball aloft like he was the Statue of Liberty. His first touchdown as a pass receiver. I knew how good it felt to him.

On the conversion try, Millersville charged like wild steers and blocked the kick. It made me wonder. Maybe I was imagining things. Maybe they were just one hell of a defensive football team.

"No way," Jake Johnson said, as we sat side by side on the bench and watched our defense get slowly steamrollered by that green machine. Foss was letting somebody else play safety. He wanted to save Jake's energy for the offense. "It's happening just like I was afraid it would. Peanuts's buddies ain't blockin' for you, man. I could see it plain on that screen pass."

47

"But how come nobody else sees it? You can't get away with a thing like that right out in broad daylight!"

"Because they wouldn't believe it even if they did see it. That's why."

"Who's in on it?"

"Wally, for sure. Burt Angstrom, for sure. And I think Bobby Johns and the Moose."

"Burt?"

"Fooled you, huh? Why do you think you can't get around right end?"

"It's hard to believe."

"Yeah. You mention it to anybody, they'll think you're paranoid or something."

"So what are we gonna do?"

"We could go to the coach. He might believe it."

"I don't want to go to the coach."

Jake lifted his shoulders.

"Don't these guys care about winning the game?"

"I guess not that much. What they care about is staying on the right side of Peanuts." He stared at the action on the field. Peanuts, from his linebacker position, had just made a great solo tackle. "Maybe they think they can win anyway."

"Maybe if I'd talk to Benny. Get him to run me at the holes where I'd get some blocking."

Jake sat silent.

"You don't think so?"

"Jack, you gotta understand. It's a funny deal. You and me, now, we can understand what's goin' down. But a kid like Benny . . . I just don't think he's ready to believe it."

A roar from the stands brought me back to the moment. Millersville had scored. A few seconds later it was 15–13, their favor. And then, just after the kickoff, the quarter ended.

We had a short huddle with our coaches. Nobody said anything important. Nobody gave me any accusing looks. Far as they were concerned, it was just another hardnosed football game.

The whole second quarter was misery—at least for me. It taught me a lesson I didn't need to learn, which is that no running back can do much against a good defense if he doesn't get that blocking. It taught me another lesson I didn't need to learn, either . . . which is how easy it is for a blocker to look like he's trying when he's not trying.

Toward the end of the half, Benny wasn't looking at me in the huddle anymore. Some of the linemen were frowning and talking to themselves . . . the ones who weren't working with Peanuts. The team was falling apart. That's what was happening, and I was sure most of them were blaming me.

I did get lucky on the last play of the half. Benny had called another long pass to Jake, this time with me as secondary receiver. I ran my route, not expecting anything, and then when I looked back, there came the ball, like that well-known bullet, dead on target. Though the cornerback hit me as I made the catch, he couldn't hold me. I went straight down the sidelines to the ten, where Jake, coming crossfield, took out the safety, and I went into the end zone for the score.

As we headed for the locker room, trailing 30–20, Benny Younger caught up with me. "I think I just woke up to something," he said.

"You did?"

"But I don't understand it."

"Yeah, well . . . I guess I don't either."

He shook his head in bewilderment. "I just don't understand it."

"Well . . . it probably ain't true, anyway."

"Sure it is." He cracked his hands together. "It's got to

49

be!" We had reached the locker room. "What'll we do?"

"I don't know. Nothin'. Maybe you can run me at different holes."

"That's not going to solve anything. I think we should go to the coach."

"Nah. I don't want to do it that way. Let's just lay back and let them hang themselves."

"But I want to win this game!" Benny stood in front of me, his eyes wild, his voice louder than he knew. "It's not just you, it's the whole team!"

"Exactly," somebody said. I looked up. It was Coach Foss. "Now sit down, Benny, and get some rest while we decide who this whole team is going to be."

I read once that the way to be heard is to speak quietly. It must be true, because Foss was speaking quietly, and all of a sudden everybody in the room was tuned in.

"You know, it's really insulting," he went on, sounding almost unconcerned, "that you birds thought you could pull something like that right in front of me and Mel and Pleasance and none of us would catch on. You, Angstrom!" His tone sharpened, turned cold. "Are you an idiot, or do you think I'm an idiot?"

Burt was round-eyed and pale. He opened his mouth; nothing came out.

"And you, Koninsberg, and Johns, and old faithful Moose Harper. What in God's name did you nitwits think you were doing out there?"

"What d'ya mean! We weren't doin' nothin'."

"That's right. And that's what you'll be doing on this team from now on."

"What d'ya mean?"

"I mean you're through. All four of you. You can ride back in the bus, but this is the last time you'll play a football game for Holbrook."

For a moment, there was nothing but silence. Then our

center, Joe Greenwood, spoke up. "Hey, coach, I don't get it. What'd these guys do?"

"They've been laying down, deliberately missing blocks, all through the first half."

"Are you serious?" Joe looked from the coach to Angstrom to Johns, back to the coach. "Why would they want to do that?"

"Ask 'em."

"He's nuts!" Bobby Johns's voice was loud, sarcastic. "What does he think, we're shavin' points or somethin'?"

"What I think isn't important," Foss said. "What I saw is important. You guys weren't blocking for Jack Delaney. Maybe I could guess why if I wanted to. Right now I don't want to."

"You know, that kind of changes it," somebody said in a careful drawl. "You're not accusing these guys of not blocking. You're accusing them of not blocking for Jack Delaney. That makes it like a conspiracy or somethin'. I don't think you got any right to say that unless you can prove it." Peanuts Gilliam. Who else? Looking at Foss with a serious face and mocking eyes.

"I don't have to prove anything, Peanuts. But since you're butting into this, I guess I will take a minute to prove something." He switched his gaze to Barney Childs, one of our cornerbacks. "What do you say, Barney? You were sitting on the bench watching our offense. Were these birds blocking for Jack?"

Barney seemed to be trying to draw his head down into his shoulders. But after a few minutes he straightened up. "It looked to me like they weren't," he said, his voice a little shaky.

"Were they blocking for Torrance?"

"Yeah. I think so."

"You, Jeff." Jeff Wagner was our middle linebacker. "What'd you see?"

"Same as Barney." Wagner didn't hesitate.

"You Sam?" Sam Burton was one of the front four, a loudmouthed kind of guy I didn't know and didn't like, even without knowing him.

"I didn't see nothin'," Burton said defiantly. "I think you're full of crap!"

"You do, hey?" Foss seemed only mildly surprised. He surveyed the rest of the team. "Anybody else think I'm full of crap?"

"Since you ask, coach," Peanuts said slowly. "Since you ask . . . yeah . . . I think you're full of crap."

Foss nodded. His expression didn't change, except for his eyes. They were narrow, glinting, hard and sharp as broken glass. I'd never seen that look before. I guess Peanuts hadn't either. He stared back for a second, then turned away, muttering something under his breath.

Foss ignored him. "We're going to play this second half," he said calmly. "And we're going to play the rest of the season. But let's line it up right now and get it over with. Either you're going to play all the way for the team and forget that follow-your-own-leader malarkey, or we don't want you. If you've got any reservations in your mind, you better go along with Peanuts and his buddies right now, 'cause you're not going to make it with the rest of us."

"Wait a minute!" Peanuts hollered. "You're not gonna lay this on me!"

"Choose your side," Foss said, ignoring him. "If you want to play, come down here. We've got work to do." He walked to the other end of the room, his two assistant coaches trailing. It was a weird scene. Could have been almost funny, if it hadn't been me that caused it. Trouble was, I felt like a fink, sitting there while the man took my part. But then I knew that wasn't true. Peanuts was a screwed-up egomaniac. I'd known a few of his kind before. Bobby Johns and that crew were just sucking along with whoever they thought was the power. I'd known that kind before, too.

I stood up and walked over to where the coaches were. Jake and Benny walked beside me. Some other guys. In a minute, when I quieted down inside and looked around, I saw that we had about twenty guys and Peanuts had the rest. Bad news. He had over half the offensive line, a good part of the defense, plus our punter, Mike Angelli.

Foss never gave that bunch another glance. "Okay," he said, "we've only got a few minutes, so we'll have to work fast." Then he stopped and started to grin, and then he was laughing. Everybody else was sort of shell-shocked and maybe half-scared and here he was, laughing like a coach with a forty-point lead.

"Hell, there's no use trying to do a lot of work" he said, scratching his head. "Let's go out there this half and have fun. Don't worry about the score. Play the best you can and don't worry." He looked us over. "We need four guys for defense. Can you play cornerback, Jack?"

I nodded.

"Who wants to try linebacker?"

That's the way it went. We patched up a team in about five minutes. Then we were back out on the field and nobody had any idea of what would happen, except we were going to get clobbered. But the amazing thing about it was that we were all high as eagles and hollering at each other and full of the kind of excitement I hadn't felt since playground ball when I was ten years old.

The Millersville team noticed right away that something had happened. When our kickoff team took the field, we had only eight men left on the bench, and three of them were so small you knew it could be against the law to let them play.

They scored on us easy, first series. I got burned on a twenty-yard pass play. We were busting our guts, but it takes more than busted guts to keep all the holes plugged.

Altogether Millersville scored four touchdowns that second half. It could have been a lot worse, believe me, if Jake hadn't intercepted a pass and Kevin Torrance, who was playing linebacker, hadn't jarred the Millersville fullback loose from the ball twice on two of the hardest hits I ever saw anybody make anywhere.

They scored four touchdowns. We scored five and a field goal. It shouldn't have happened, couldn't have happened, but it did. Maybe because we were so loose we never stopped to think about all the reasons it couldn't happen.

Like on our first play from scrimmage. Jeff Wagner was playing right tackle for us. In the huddle he said, "I don't know the plays. Just tell me who to block."

"Take the man in front of you to the inside," Benny told him, then called my number on the off-tackle dive. I went through the biggest hole I'd seen all game and kept going for forty yards.

"Everybody out for a pass," Benny said. "Linemen, don't try to knock your man down, just hold him off." The Millersville secondary got confused, probably because we had three receivers in the same zone. Benny hit Jake on the twenty, and Jake went in standing up.

And that's the way it went. They'd score and then we'd score. We practically threw away the playbook. Benny'd say, "Jack's going through the three hole, on two. Jeff, you let your man in. Go by him and knock down the middle linebacker." Jeff would do it, and after I busted through the line I'd see daylight. There's nothing better in the world than that feeling when you find yourself loose in the secondary, and you've got a guy like Jake out there in front of you to make the one block you really need.

It wasn't all just Jake and Benny and me and the blockers. Torrance gained over fifty yards, running inside. Our little split end, Chris Buchanan, scored a touchdown on an end-around we made up in the huddle. Benny didn't throw much. He didn't have to, the way our ground game was going. The whole second half was like one of those dreams where the kid comes off the bench and makes the eighty-yard run to win the game. Only this time it was like every one of us was that kid. We were all doing things better than we knew how, and toward the end we were even getting together on the defense.

After it was over, we piled into the bus. We'd shower and change at Holbrook. "Peanuts must've hired a couple of taxis to get those guys back," somebody said. And that was all. We weren't interested in Peanuts and his troubles. We were interested in ourselves, in our team. It was a hell of a feeling. I'd played on a few teams before, but for the first time in my life I was *in* a team. There wasn't a lot of hollering or horseplay. Even the coaches were quiet—or maybe just dazed. We had started out that morning with thirty football players. We were coming home with nineteen.

The numbers didn't matter. Even the numbers in the score didn't matter. What mattered was the game and the way we had played it. I suddenly saw the game—any game—as a kind of abstraction, a form that is always there. You climb up into the structure of the game and you begin by going through certain formal motions; and then when things are right, it all changes and you really begin to *play,* almost like dancing without thoughts, like music that carries you away. For a little while you *are* the game, and when you do it that way the score doesn't matter.

Of course, at the end the score does matter—more to some players than to others, sometimes more to the watchers than to any of the players. But as far as the game itself is concerned, nothing has changed. The game remains, waiting for the next players.

These were some of the things I started to understand

after the Millersville game. Not all of them, not all at once, and they didn't stay with me all the time; but they were nice ideas to come back to when things got confusing.

7

"Heard you had quite a day today." As usual my uncle Fred had saved his conversation till supper time.

"Uh . . . yeah, pretty good."

"Heard you practically beat Millersville single-handed."

"Where'd you hear that baloney?"

"Well, I'll tell you, I heard it from Corwin Williams. And Corwin Williams is not what you'd call a baloney slicer."

"Who is this guy Corwin Williams? I remember you were quoting him last week, too."

"That's right. And you remember what he said, too, don't you?"

"Well, I sure didn't win any game single-handed. Nobody wins a football game single-handed."

"Corwin says you gained about four hundred yards and played defense and did the punting and threw a pass for a touchdown and I don't know what-all. He said you were the first triple-threat player he'd seen in action in twenty years."

"He musta been watching some other game."

"What's a triple-threat player?" Aunt Frieda asked.

"That's a player who can do everything. When you're on the other side, it feels like you're playing against triplets. Ain't that right, Jack?"

"You and Corwin Williams are both full of baloney."

"Is that so?" But he was grinning. "Score was 59–58.

Sounds like a basketball score. Corwin says you made the winning touchdown with only eight seconds to play.''

"Me and ten other guys."

"Sure. Corwin says you scored five touchdowns, and some of the time you didn't have ten other guys helping you."

"Five touchdowns!" Aunt Frieda shook her head in wonder. "My, that sounds like a lot."

"You better believe it's a lot. Corwin Williams says that Jack is the best high school football player he ever saw. What d'ya think of that!"

"Why, I think it's wonderful. I never dreamed you were such a good athlete, Jack."

I looked down at my plate, which was full of mashed potatoes and pork loin. What the hell was this? Me getting all choked up over a few kind words?

We had squash pie with whipped cream on it for dessert. Some kind of good. I had two pieces. And was starting to think about something else when Uncle Fred said, "One thing really puzzled Corwin, though. He says part of the team didn't show up for the second half. Thought there might have been an argument or somethin'. What was that all about, Jack?"

"Aaah . . . just a hassle. Coach thought some of the guys weren't doin' their best, and they didn't like it, and I guess he sort of kicked 'em off the team."

"Sort of, huh? Was Wilbur Gilliam's boy mixed up in it?"

"You mean Peanuts?"

"I guess they do call him Peanuts. His real name is Derek."

"I never heard anybody call him that."

"But he was one of 'em?"

"Yeah."

"Wilbur ain't gonna like that." Uncle Fred whistled. "Man alive, he is really not going to like that."

"Who is he? I mean I heard somebody say he owned half the town."

"Oh, I wouldn't say that. Prob'ly only a third. Prob'ly could buy the whole town if he wanted to, though."

"How come a rich guy like that's living here in Holbrook?"

"Well, it ain't the worst place in the world. And then there's that thing about bein' a real big frog in a middle-sized puddle. Some folks ain't happy unless they can feel like real big frogs."

"I don't think Wilbur's as bad as you make him out to be, Fred." Aunt Frieda had to feel strongly about a thing before she'd disagree with her husband at the supper table.

"I don't make him out to be bad. I just make him out to be a jackass."

"Well, I don't know about that!" Aunt Frieda was not so mild now. "All I know is he's made an awful lot of money, and far as I can see he never hurt anybody doing it, either."

"Wilbur used to be sweet on your aunt," Uncle Fred said with a wink. "She's never stopped kicking her own behind for turning him down."

"That's not true!" My aunt's face was flushed. For a moment I could see the kind of girl she must have been thirty years ago. "I've never regretted it for a minute."

"I know, sweetie, I know. I was just teasin'." Sometimes my uncle was just a kid, too. The more I saw of the two of them, the more I liked them. And the less sure I was of what I thought I knew about them.

"But you know, yourself," Uncle Fred went on, "Wilbur actually ain't got enough sense to pound salt up a rathole. If his daddy hadn't left him a couple a million to play around with them copper mines out West, he'd prob'ly be waitin' on trade for me down at the hardware."

"Well, if you aren't . . . !" Aunt Frieda left the rest of it unsaid. She turned to me. "What kind of a boy is Derek . . . Peanuts? I heard he was kind of wild."

"He's a spoiled brat, that's what he is," Uncle Fred volunteered.

"I wasn't asking *you*!"

"I know you weren't. I just thought I'd give you the benefit of my expert opinion." Uncle Fred pushed back his chair. "I'm gonna read my paper. Give you two a chance to gossip about the rich folks."

"Really, Jack, what kind of a boy is he?" Aunt Frieda rested her elbows on the table and cupped her chin in her two hands. She wasn't a gossip, but she did love to talk, or rather to have conversations. To tell the truth, I liked to talk to her, too. We'd been developing sort of a habit lately. When I'd get home from practice, she'd have coffee or milk and maybe some sweet rolls she'd baked or a sandwich ready for a snack before supper, and we'd sit at the big kitchen table and talk about what I'd been doing in school or maybe about what the rain was doing to the rhubarb. I mean, nothing important. But the talking itself was important—at least to me. In the old days my mom and I used to talk sometimes, but she was usually at me about something, or else she was worrying about the welfare and different problems she had.

With Aunt Frieda, it was different. The kitchen was warm, and I was tired from practice and we were getting used to each other, so there wasn't any strain between us and . . . well, it was getting to where that hour before supper was one of the best parts of the day for me.

"I don't know that much about him," I said. "He seems all right." She waited patiently, as she always did, for more. "Well, to be honest about it, Peanuts and I don't get along. A personality conflict, I guess you could call it."

"Mmmm." She said "mmmm" a lot when she was

listening. Sometimes she said "mmm-hmmm," kind of rising on the second part.

"It's too bad," she said. "Fred's probably right in a way. Only child . . . too much money and too little discipline. I know it's old-fashioned, but I don't think it's good for children to let them run loose."

Maybe she saw something in my look, because she said, "Oh, I don't mean you, Jack! I mean somebody like Wilbur's boy, who could have almost anything in the world he wanted just by asking for it. Except possibly the one thing he wanted most. You see, when he was little his parents traveled a good deal. He was left at home with a housekeeper and a nursemaid. And then his mother died . . . and his father got married again, then divorced, and remarried." She shook her head. "Sounds like a classic story of the poor little rich boy, doesn't it?"

"Mmmm."

"I know. You don't think that's any excuse for somebody turning into a brat. And I guess it isn't." She smiled, a little wistful and sad. "I wonder why it is that a thing that looks so good to one person can turn out to be so bad for another."

"You mean like money?"

"Money . . . or success . . . sometimes what we see as freedom . . . or even getting your heart's desire."

"Was I your heart's desire, sweetie?" Uncle Fred called from the living room.

"Was I yours?" she said, without raising her voice.

"You bet, and you still are."

Afterwards, while I was changing my clothes to go to the dance, I wondered about it. Had he really been her heart's desire? And she his? Probably . . . at the time. She had chosen him over the rich man. Why? Looking at him now it was hard to tell. Except for a certain quality, a kind of unsinkable spirit, something light and bright that still flashed in his eyes and rang sometimes like bells in the ordinary sound of his words. And I realized more than ever before how impossible it is to really know much about what goes on deep inside another person. Unless you're very close to him or her for a long time . . . and even then you can never be sure.

One thing I liked about living with my aunt and uncle was having my own room. I'd been living for so long in a dormitory with sixty or seventy other guys that I'd forgotten what it was like to have a room of your own where it was dark and quiet at night—a room you could go into and close the door and be alone with yourself for as long as you wanted. Learning to live again in the free world was not an easy trip for me. Having a room where I could go and think things over was a big help.

It was a square, medium-sized, kind of old-fashioned bedroom with cream-colored walls and a light-blue braided oval rug on a brown painted wood floor. Before I came, I suppose it had been the "spare" room. My aunt and uncle had never had any children. It was something they didn't talk about, and of course I didn't ask.

The room had a big closet, which looked bare with the amount of clothes I had hanging in it. Not that it mattered much. I wasn't used to having more than two pairs of pants, anyway. Aunt Frieda had offered to buy me a suit, but I'd said I'd wait till I needed one. Tonight I sort of wished I had that suit. The best I could put together for the dance was a pair of straight-leg tan corduroys and a white shirt and a dark-blue V-neck sweater. They were actually the best clothes I had ever owned, all clean and new; and after I put them on and looked at myself in the mirror over the dresser, I thought I looked okay. I was starting to feel very good. A little scared, but mostly good. This would be the first real dance I had ever been to—and Cindy Farr would be there. And, naturally, as soon as I started to think about her, I started to get nervous. What would she think about a guy coming to a dance in corduroy pants and a sweater? Oh, boy. That kind of thinking was no good.

I turned out the light in my room and clomped down the stairs, my new loafers a little tight on my feet.

"Oh, you look just fine, Jack!" Aunt Frieda said. "Doesn't he look fine, Fred?"

"Fine as elderberry wine." My uncle grinned and tipped me a wink. "Have yourself a time," he said.

I said I would and I said good-night, and then I got out of there. I didn't know if I ever again would get used to living in a house where there was so much love and good feeling flying around.

Walking downtown to the youth center, I felt myself starting to stiffen up a little and ache in a few places from the pounding I'd taken that afternoon. So I trotted and swung my arms and tried most of all to get my head loose and easy, like it had been when we started the second half.

The youth center was in the business district. It had been a store once. The show windows were now painted over and the counters, or whatever had been in there, replaced by Ping-Pong and pool tables and pinball machines you could play for a dime. Tonight everything had been pushed to the walls, leaving a big open space for dancing. Too open, was my first feeling. I was wishing for a few dark corners, where a guy could stand sort of invisibly and get himself together.

No way to be invisible tonight, though. The place was jammed, music booming from a couple of huge speakers at the end of the room. As I tried to edge my way around the dance floor, it seemed like everybody I bumped into was saying, "Hey, man, great game!"

"Thought you weren't going to be that football hero!"

I looked down—and into the blue slanty eyes of Lori Curtin.

"I . . . uh. . . ."

"I know. You . . . uh. . . . Listen, Jack, how about dancing with me before the cheerleaders spot you and start tearing your clothes off."

"You're nuts."

"So? You afraid to dance with a nut?"

"I told you, I don't know how to dance."

"Oh, my God." She rolled her eyes. "C'mon. If you wait another minute you may never get a chance to learn." She grabbed my hand, and before I knew what was happening I was out on the dance floor. She was looking up at me, smiling. "Just let the music move you," she said. "It's easy."

I didn't believe it. But I was out there. And I could feel the beat of the music, all right. And Lori Curtin had the kind of confidence that's contagious. We were dancing. Or that's the way it felt, anyway.

The record ended with a crash. Everybody stopped. I looked around, spotted Benny Younger and Linda Gerhardt standing by the wall in a group of five or six, and the only one of the group who was looking at me was—you know it—Cindy Farr.

"Listen, I gotta talk to a friend," I said to Lori. "It was great dancing with you."

"Sure. That's why you've got to talk to a friend."

Lori's all right, I was thinking as I pushed my way through the crowd toward Cindy. Too good a girl to spend her time with a mutt like Peanuts Gilliam.

Just as I reached Cindy's group, the music started again. Elton John this time, wailing like a lost soul. Cindy was talking to Linda. Benny was talking to some guy I didn't know. I said, "Hi," but nobody heard me through the music. I stood there for a second, feeling the same old helplessness. I just wasn't any good at trying to force my way into social situations.

Then Cindy turned and looked at me and said, "Hello, Jack." She wasn't smiling. Her eyes were huge and serious and she was so beautiful I knew I'd never stand a chance with her.

"Hi." I tried to grin. I could feel my head nodding like an idiot's. Could feel sudden sweat running down my side under my shirt.

"Hey, old Jackeroo!" Benny was flushed, bright-eyed, hyper as a guy discovering the North Pole. For a second I thought he might be drunk or on speed or something. But that wouldn't be like Benny. He was probably just high on himself and the music and the people and, yeah, memories of the game.

"Let's do it!" he said, and he and Linda disappeared in the swirl of dancers. I was left alone with Cindy Farr. Alone with two hundred other people, but at that moment I wasn't aware of any of them.

"How's things?"

"Oh. . . ." She smiled then, her quirky, funny-face smile that took away my breath. "Things are all right. How're things with you?"

"Okay. I mean, great. It's good to see you again."

"It's good to see you again, too." Still smiling, calm, and sort of waiting, she was looking at me.

"I . . . uh . . . I'd ask you to dance, but I really don't even know how to dance."

"Oh?"

"Well, I . . . believe it or not, that's the first time I ever actually danced with anybody."

"Would you like to try again?"

"Yeah."

64

So we did. And I couldn't tell you what it was like, I mean whether I was dancing or walking around in circles or standing on my head. All I knew was I was out there with her, sometimes touching, sometimes not, looking into her eyes, smelling her warmth, feeling her grace, her good strong body.

We danced for quite a while. Nobody else said anything to us. If they did I didn't hear them. All of a sudden it was intermission, or some kind of a break. Everybody stopped dancing and started milling around two tables along the wall, where people were handing out Cokes and coffee and cake and stuff. An older guy stood up on a chair and gave a short speech welcoming the crowd to the youth center. Then he reminded everybody that the goodies didn't fall from heaven, and contributions would be appreciated.

I reached into my pocket . . . and found out I didn't have a nickel. Not unusual for me, but embarrassing just the same. Uncle Fred had been slipping me a few bucks every week as a kind of allowance. I always felt guilty taking it and had been trying to find a way to earn some money of my own. Football practice every afternoon made it hard to find a part-time job, but a supermarket manager had told me he might need a bag boy in the evenings soon. All this was running through my mind when Cindy said, "Here, I've got a dollar. Let's put that in."

"You put it in." I knew it was stupid to worry about a dollar, and especially whether she put it in or I put it in.

"Hey, you want to borrow five bucks, hotshot?" Peanuts Gilliam was standing right behind us, hands in his pockets, a kind of innocent smirk on his face.

For a second I honest-to-God couldn't believe he was doing something like that. I stared at him. He stared back. Then he switched his gaze to Cindy for a long appraising look. She didn't know what was going on. I could feel her looking at me, wondering.

"No," I said. "Thanks, anyway." I turned away from him. My face felt pale.

"Why do you have to be such a bastard!" It was Lori Curtin's voice, behind us.

"Just trying to be helpful," Peanuts said, loud and slurry. Sounded like he might be drunk. "Figured ole hotshot might want to buy his girl an ice-cream soda."

Inside, everything was tightening up, slowing down, stopping. I knew what was going to happen, and I didn't want it to happen—not here, not this way. But now everything had stopped, dead center, and when it started to move again it was going to move in only one direction.

Cindy touched my arm. "Jack, let's get out of here." Her eyes were wide and worried. She didn't need to know the details to feel something bad in the air. "It's not worth it," she said. "Let's get out of here."

"Okay." I couldn't get into a fight in front of her, so I said okay and stepped straight ahead without seeing anything, and bumped smack into somebody else.

"Hey, don't let that punk run you out, baby!" It was Jake Johnson, serious and hard in a way I'd never seen him. "We'll run him out if it gets down to that."

And on the instant some band or strap broke inside me. I was back in the room again and I could see everything and I was loose . . . and I started to laugh. I couldn't help it. Cindy pulling me out of trouble. And Jake wanting to take care of me . . . it was too much. It was great.

"We were leaving anyway," I said to Jake. "Hey, thanks, man . . . everything's cool."

Even when we got outside, I couldn't stop laughing.

"Maybe it's a release from nervous tension," I said to Cindy.

She didn't answer me. We were walking along Main Street, past lighted store windows. I turned to look at her. She was staring straight ahead, marching like a soldier.

"What's the matter?"

"Nothing."

We kept walking for a while, not very far, about half a block.

"Well, something must be the matter."

"Why would you think something's the matter?"

"I don't know. I mean we're not talking or anything."

"We're talking."

"Hey. . . ." I stopped in the middle of the sidewalk and turned to face her. She kept right on walking. I caught up with her. "Hey . . . come on . . . what're you mad about?"

She kept her face straight ahead . . . but it wasn't a straight face any more. She was giggling. She flashed me one of her special looks . . . lips pressed tight to keep from laughing, but her eyes and her whole face alight.

"Hey!"

She stopped and looked at me with that sudden seriousness that always made something inside me jump up into my throat.

"You're the greatest girl I've ever known in my life."

"I guess you haven't known too many girls."

She was like that. . . . I was beginning to understand. If you said something nice to her, or something you thought was nice, she would turn it away with the first thing that came into her mind.

"Oh, I didn't mean that!" she said. "I *was* mad for a minute, because I thought you were laughing at me and at that other boy—laughing at us because we thought we were doing the right thing."

"You thought I needed help, didn't you?"

"I guess . . . something like that."

"Well, I did. I'd have gotten myself in a mess if it hadn't been for you. But I was laughing at . . . I don't know exactly . . . it just felt so good all of a sudden to know that you and Jake were trying to take care of me . . . and to realize that the whole trouble was my own stupidity, letting that creep, Peanuts, bug me.''

"It's not your stupidity." She was giving me that serious look. "You expect too much of yourself, you know."

Oh, and there it was again. Certain things people could say to me. Certain kinds of understanding things . . . certain kinds of *kind* things . . . and I'd get that damned knot in my throat.

"Do you know about me being in Marshfield?"

"I know you were there. That's all."

"Well, how do you feel about that?"

"Jack, I don't feel anything about it. I mean it doesn't affect me one way or the other."

"It has to affect you some way."

"You think it does, and I guess I can't blame you for thinking that, but it really doesn't."

"Don't you want to know what I was in for?"

"I don't think it matters to me. But maybe it would. I don't know." She put her hand on my arm. We stopped at a corner. We were out of the business district now, but there was a streetlight and I could see her clearly, looking at me, her brows drawn in a puzzled frown. "It's a hard thing," she said, "but I don't think you should put questions like that to people. I mean you're trying to clear everything up before anything even gets started. You must know I have a good feeling about you or I wouldn't be out here with you."

"Yeah, but I don't want you to think I'm something that I'm not."

"You know what it is, Jack? Most people, when they meet another person they think they might like, put their best side out in front, hoping the other person will like them too. They know that after a while the other person will see some of the bad side, because everybody's got a bad side, but they hope that by then the other person will

68

like them enough, so the bad side won't matter that much. Why should you feel you have to go about it just the opposite, just because you've been in Marshfield? Some of the worst people in the world never go to jail, you know."

I couldn't answer her. I understood what she was saying. In a way, I did.

"You'll tell me all about it sometime." She was smiling now. "There's no rush."

God. This girl. There wasn't anybody in the world like this girl. I was so full of love for her I wanted to do some great impossible thing to show her how I felt. Rescue her from a burning house . . . risk my life in a raging flood . . . lose my life . . . anything.

What I did, of course, was another piece of Jack Delaney dumbness.

"I guess I was worried you might get in trouble going out with somebody with a record."

"What? How could I get in trouble?"

"I mean that school for girls. I thought they might have some rule against it."

"C.S.G?" She stared at me, her eyes slowly widening. "Wait a minute! You think Columbus School for Girls . . . ? What kind of school do you think that is?"

"I don't know." I was getting a very bad feeling. "Some kind of a school for girls."

"Oh, brother! That's what it is." She was shaking her head, laughing and crying. "But not what you think, Jack. Not a reform school. Is that what you think?"

"I thought it was something like that."

"Oh, Lord! It's a private school! An expensive private school. I go there because my parents want me to, and I go because I think I'm getting a better education there than I would in public school. But maybe I'm not. It's a very good school, and I'm not knocking it, but I have all kinds of mixed emotions about it. Sometimes I feel guilty about being able to go there just because my parents can afford to pay for it. It's not fair. But I go anyway. And I'm apologetic about it . . . . You know, it's amazing. I'm almost as defensive about C.S.G. as you are about Marshfield!"

It was amazing, all right. Amazing how I could be so wrong about so many things in one single damned day.

"Oh, come on!" she said. "It's funny, Jack. It's really funny!"

And all of a sudden it was. Another twisted hunk of iron—that's what it felt like—came spinning out of my head. I was laughing again and she was laughing and I leaned forward and bent down a little bit and kissed her.

She was looking at me with a look I'd never seen anywhere. "It's not funny anymore, is it?"

"No. But it's the best thing I ever felt in my life."

"Me, too."

We started walking again. She took my hand. We didn't talk. I was full to the top of my head with the best feeling I'd ever had in my life.

School on Monday was different from the first minute. People were saying hello to me, looking at me. I could hear the different tones in their voices, feel their eyes. It wasn't imagination or delusion or anything like that. A couple of little kids—they must have been ninth-graders, but they really looked like little kids—stopped me in the hall and asked how many touchdowns I was going to score against Blanton. I didn't even know what Blanton was.

"That's your next game, man!" one of them told me.

Then, nudging his friend, "This guy don't care *who* he plays!"

I guess it was my first taste of what you could call football-hero baloney. I'd be lying if I didn't say a part of me ate it up. Sure, I knew it was baloney, and I knew that baloney all by itself won't even make a good sandwich. But when you're hungry, you'll go for the baloney—and don't let anybody tell you otherwise.

Some of the girls were giving me a smile, too, which no doubt would have been more important to me if it had happened last week before Cindy Farr wiped out practically all my interest in any girl-smiles but hers. Cindy Farr. I'd be looking at Mrs. Swanson in science class, and there'd come Cindy, real as life, blocking all the space between me and the teacher. Once in the hall I saw a girl disappear around a corner, and for an instant I was sure it was Cindy. It was like a super-flood of adrenalin: shaky knees, tight belly, dry mouth. God! It was like soap-opera stories of first love. I'd never believed that stuff before, I mean that it could hit you that hard. Why did she have to be way down in Columbus? She wasn't even sure she could get to Holbrook next weekend. She was supposed to go somewhere with her parents. How could I wait two weeks to see her again? I couldn't. That's all. I'd have to get down to Columbus somehow, if only to see her for an hour.

Practice that afternoon was like starting a new season. Six of us would be going both ways, offense and defense. We all had a lot to learn about playing our new positions. For instance, the first thing I had to learn about playing cornerback was that covering your man was only part of it. Everything depended on field position. Sometimes it was better to give the offense the short gainers. Sounded simple, but as Coach Foss put it, the thing that was apt to mess you up was your own ego. Worry too much about getting beat on the short ones, and sooner or later you'd get burned on a long one. It was hard work for all of us, going back to fundamentals we had never really learned. It was good, too, because the spirit was good and we were all working together, for each other and for the team in a way that makes football become the game you thought it might be when you first went out to play.

Then on Tuesday afternoon we got a small shock. Cal Pleasance quit as assistant coach, supposedly because he'd found he couldn't spare the time from his drugstore. Rumor, though, had it that Pleasance had resigned rather than risk losing favor with Peanuts Gilliam's father, who owned part of the bank that was lending the money for remodeling the Pleasance drugstore. Complicated, and hard to believe.

"Not hard to believe," Jake Johnson told me, "not if you understand how things work in a small town. Everything's tied together. Like, old man Gilliam is on the school board, and if you see a worried look on the coach's face you can figure that one out, too."

"Aaah, come on! People can't be that petty."

Jake shrugged. "You'd be surprised."

That night when I mentioned it at the supper table, my uncle Fred gave me a squinch-eyed look and said, "I'd hate to believe he could be that petty, too, Jack, but your friend put his finger on somethin'. Folks magnify things sometimes, specially small-town folks. They let things get all out of proportion, maybe because there ain't enough other stuff going on to keep 'em occupied. Like the time Sam Donalds sued Mort Grabowski for an easement on that old——"

"Nonsense!" Aunt Frieda interrupted. "Wilbur Gilliam may have his faults, but he's not a mean or vindictive man, Fred Delaney, and you know that as well as I do!"

"I grant you, but—on the other hand—he'd do most anything for that boy of his, and you know *that* as well as I do." He turned his attention back to me. "There's already lots of talk all over town about Peanuts getting kicked off the team. Brewing up to be a regular tempest in a teapot, looks like. But your aunt's probably right. Chances are Wilbur don't even know a thing about it yet. He's always got his head off in a dream somewhere. So best thing's don't pay any attention to what you hear. Ninety-eight percent of it'll be pure horse manure."

"I just hope Coach Foss won't get any pressure. He's a good guy. And he didn't have any choice."

"It'll all blow over in a week or two," Uncle Fred said. "Meantime, you stick with Joe Foss. Corwin Williams was telling me today that if you keep playing like you started, you'll have fifty colleges offering you a scholarship. What d'ya think of that!"

I shook my head and ate my pie. Lemon meringue this time. Aunt Frieda was some kind of pie baker.

Nothing much happened on Wednesday, except that I lost my cap. It was just an old leather cap I liked to wear sometimes, and I was pretty sure I'd had it when I went to the locker room, but then after practice I couldn't find it. No big deal. I kind of hated to lose it, though, even if it was too small. It was about the only thing I had left that my mother had given me. Well, maybe it'd turn up . . . damn sure nothing anybody'd want to steal.

One other thing that happened Wednesday. Somebody put a poster up on the main bulletin board. It said: NO PEP RALLY THIS WEEK. FREAKY FOSS HAS FOULED US FOR FAIR. Only it didn't say "fouled." It didn't stay on the board long. I didn't even see it, but the whole school was talking about it. Later in the day a couple more NO PEP RALLY signs were put up and torn down.

"This is not good news," Benny Younger said in the locker room. "I heard some guys talking against the team. I couldn't believe they were serious."

"Benny, you are a very sweet person," Jake Johnson

said, "but sometimes you remind me of one of the Rover Boys."

"Who're they?"

"Or maybe the Hardy Boys."

"Oh, yeah?" Benny reddened. "Well, I think school spirit's important, and I don't dig people trying to tear it down."

"Me, too, baby. But what'd you expect Peanuts'd be doing . . . leading the cheers?"

"How do you know it's Peanuts?"

"How do I know clouds cause rain?"

Benny laughed, which didn't necessarily mean he was convinced. It just wasn't his nature to believe anything bad about anybody until he had proof.

We had another good practice, anyway. Nobody else on the team was taking the posters very seriously, and I wasn't either. Maybe it was Peanuts, maybe it wasn't. The whole thing seemed childish, whichever way you looked at it.

Thursday we had another piece of bad news. Terry Webster quit the team. Terrible Terry, they called him, because he was five-feet-five and weighed one-thirty and had a face that was prettier than ninety percent of the girls in school. But he was a deadly tackler and, with the shape the team was in now, we were going to miss him in the secondary.

"He said he had to help his old man after school." Barney Childs was sitting on the bench in front of his locker, one shoe on and one shoe off, gloomily inspecting a huge hole in his sock. "Things keep goin', we won't have eleven guys left."

"Funny he never had to help him before," Joe Green-wood said. Joe was playing in the defensive line now, as well as his regular center position. He had a couple of big new bruises on his arms and wasn't totally happy about being a workhorse.

"Maybe his old man owes the bank some money." This, with a grin, from Jeff Wagner. Jeff was going both ways, too—linebacker and offensive guard—and loving every head-knocking minute of it.

"Come on, you guys!" Benny Younger said. "Let's not be making a big plot out of everything that happens. Personally, I think Terry was taking too much punishment out there. He's not built for it."

"None of 'em got it right," Jake Johnson said to me afterward. "Terrible Terry is a kid who likes to party. I mean the kind of partying Peanuts and his gang go for. So he decided he'd rather party than play football. That's the way I see it."

Maybe so. It didn't matter to me, except it was too bad everything had to split on such a heavy seam. You could see it happening all through the school. The Peanuts people making cracks at the team people, and vice versa. A lot of the kids who lined up on Peanuts's side were the kind who liked to think they were hip, cool, too sophisticated maybe to go to football games. In principle I sometimes felt a little closer to them than I did to a lot of the upright types who were on "our" side. The Mr. Cleans of the world and their sisters, the Ms. Sparklebrights, can be boring at times.

Even the teachers started getting into the act. Mrs. Swanson, the science teacher, didn't pussyfoot around. On Friday she announced to each of her classes that she was going to the game tomorrow, and she expected to see all of her students there. Not only see them there but hear them . . . rooting for Holbrook. "In my opinion," she said, "football is neither more nor less silly than most of the other games people play. And I'll admit that I sometimes don't go to a single game all season. But this school is important to me and you people who make up the school are important to me, and I can't sit quiet now and watch you divide yourselves into factions simply because a few headstrong people don't like the way the team is being run.''

She paused, out of breath, and tried to tuck some willful wisps of hair back into the bun on top of her head. She had great intentions and I had to give her credit, especially if what Jake had said was true . . . I mean about Peanuts's old man being a power on the school board. But she wasn't a very good practical psychologist. The Peanuts people just laughed at her. And she may even have given them an idea they wouldn't have thought of by themselves.

Because when we trotted out on the field for Saturday's game against Blanton, we were greeted with what sounded at first like a whole lot more boos than cheers. It stopped us for a second. Nobody likes to be booed, especially on his home turf.

The field at Holbrook had a concrete grandstand along one sideline and temporary wooden bleachers along the other. For our first game that season, against Kirby, the grandstand which was for the home-side rooters, had been about half full and the bleachers practically empty. Today we were playing to a packed house. At first I thought the bleachers must be full of kids from Blanton—they did have two cheerleaders over there. While we were warming up, though, the guys on our team kept staring at those bleachers and shaking their heads and muttering, and pretty soon I began to get the picture. The bleachers were full of Blanton rooters all right, except that most of them were kids from Holbrook.

"Did you spot Peanuts yet?" Jake Johnson asked me.

"Uh-uh."

"He's right on their fifty-yard line. Him and Burt and Bobby Johns and the whole crew and a bunch of girls. And there's plenty of grown-ups from Holbrook over there, too.''

"Well, maybe they couldn't find any place else to sit.''

"Maybe . . some of 'em. He shook his head, scowl-ing. "I didn't think it'd be this bad."

A Blanton cheer came rolling across the field. As we gathered around Coach Foss for our usual pre-game psych-up, our guys kept twisting their heads, looking at the bleachers, trying to figure out exactly what was happening.

"Put it out of your minds!" Foss said sharply. "We're here to play football. We don't give a damn about who's sitting on which side of the field. Now do we?"

"No!"

"I said, *do we*?"

"*No!*" The answer came loud and sharp this time. It was the old coaching trick, getting the team to answer emotional questions as a group, getting them hyped up, full of the old all-for-one-one-for-all baloney. Only, of course, it's not just baloney, not once you flow with it and let the spirit grab you.

We took the kickoff, paying no attention to anything but the goal line, and in five plays we had our first touchdown. Blanton wasn't good enough to stop us, and it probably wouldn't have mattered who was full of what old spirit. They weren't good enough to run against us either. On top of that, their passing game was weak. At the end of the quarter it was 14–0. By halftime we were on top, 27–6, and we all knew—our team and the Blanton team—that this game was a mismatch. Still, you can't let down even in a game like that, because all it takes is a few fumbles and a few breaks and everything can get turned around.

The biggest contest all through the half had actually been between the two cheering sections. God knows what the real Blanton rooters thought was happening, but their cheerleaders had obviously decided not to look any gift horses in the mouth. They'd wait for the Holbrook side to finish a cheer and then back they'd come with a "*Gi'me a*

B. . . . Gi'me an L . . . ," and so on. Anybody from outside seeing the game would have thought we were playing for at least the state championship.

In the locker room at halftime, Coach Foss didn't say much. He looked a little white around the mouth, though, and you could almost see the wheels whirring in his head.

When we went back on the field, the noise seemed to have quieted down a bit. The teams lined up for the kick-off. I was sitting on the bench. Kickoff team was the only one I didn't play on. Then, just as the referee blew his whistle, something happened in the bleachers across the field. Five or six people stood up and unfurled a big banner . . . a big sign. . . .

Our kicker, little Teddy Aronson, had already sent the ball arching toward the Blanton goal line, and things were happening out there on the field, but all I could see was this sign:

HOLBROOK IS *WHOLE*BROOK
NOT JACK, JAKE, AND JOEBROOK

The rest of the game was dull. Nobody could concentrate. I mean, on our side. It didn't matter much, because Blanton didn't have the horses. We scored twice. They scored once. So we won it, 40–13. And it all added up to a big bagful of nothing. For me, anyway.

"So, to hell with it." Jake and Benny and I and a few other guys were sitting around in the locker room. Jake was talking. "We won. That's what counts, right?"

"Sure," somebody said.

Benny was sitting there, looking puzzled. "It's really weird. Why are we bugging ourselves this way?"

"I don't know. I never did believe in that old school-spirit crap." Jeff Wagner slowly pulled on his blue nylon windbreaker.

"Maybe it's because all those girls were rooting against us," Benny said. "I never thought the girls would go against us."

"It was only a few," Jake said. "Those kind of girls go wherever the wind blows them."

"Yeah." We all sat and thought about it for a while.

"Most of the girls were on our side," Jake said.

"Maybe most. But a whole lot were with Peanuts and Bobby Johns." Benny couldn't get over it. "I just don't understand how they could be so bitchy."

"Hey, man. Some girls are bitchy. And witchy." Jake was grinning. "Course I ain't the one to speak about your white ladies. But women are women. That's one thing I know. And some of them can be just as evil as men and maybe eviler. And it don't do no good to sit around and say, 'How could they *do* that?' "

"You know, one funny thing. . . ." It was the first time Barney Childs had opened his mouth. "Lori Curtin was sitting on our side. I saw her with Midge Gallup and that bunch."

"What's so funny about that?" Jake asked, with too much innocence.

"Come on! You know how tight she's always been with Peanuts."

"Well, I guess she found some good reason to switch sides." Jake was looking at me, grinning that big slow grin of his, and I realized they were all looking at me. I felt like a ten-year-old, really embarrassed. I just looked at my shoes. One thing I knew: I didn't want to be the reason for Lori Curtin's switching sides. But at the same time—and I guess it's that old male-ego baloney—I have to admit I felt a little push of something else. And when I looked up I was grinning. I knew I was being a real horse's ass. But I couldn't help it.

10

Monday morning the roof of the world caved in. The roof of my world, anyway. I got to school early and first thing I noticed was how many kids were standing around in little knots and groups, talking to each other. No movement through the halls, just everybody standing still, talking, and gesturing.

As I passed a couple of these groups and saw some people I knew, I nodded and said, "Hi," and they said, "Hi," back; but their eyes were wide and I could feel something coming out of them: a question, an excitement, maybe almost a fear.

I went to my homeroom. It was empty. I mean, no people. That's when I knew something very big was happening. It was only ten minutes to first bell, and there should have been at least fifteen or twenty kids in homeroom, some flipping pages in a desperate effort to make up for studying they should have done yesterday, the others socializing in different ways, depending on what they were after.

I walked over to my seat, put my books down, and stood there for a minute, wondering. And I started to have a bad feeling. Something was going on and it had to do with me. Because I was standing here all by myself, and everybody else was out there in the halls, talking to one another.

"Hi, Jack."

I turned around. It was Lori Curtin. She had a tense look on her face, staring at me, not playing any eye games now.

"You don't know what happened, do you?"

"No."

"I *know* you don't. But it's going to be a bitch, Jack, I'll tell you."

"What is?"

She swallowed, and then spoke with an effort. "The principal's office was broken into over the weekend. They took some money."

"So?"

"So. . . ." She hesitated, and shook her head in a kind of helpless anger. "So they found a cap in there, and it's supposed to be yours."

"Mine?" I didn't get it. And then I did. "Oh, boy,"

"That little leather cap of yours. Have you still got it?"

"I lost it a couple weeks ago."

"You're being framed, baby." And there was Jake Johnson, standing right beside Lori. I hadn't even seen him enter the room. My mind was very slow. All I could think of was that this must be what it felt like to have tunnel vision.

"Why would anybody want to frame me?" I honest-to-God couldn't believe it. It was like I was in some very bad old movie, *Bowery Boys Try to Make Good,* or something.

"Jake! You think *Peanuts* did it?" Lori sounded like she thought it was a bad movie, too.

"Who else? I mean anybody might try to rob the school, but who else would want to frame Jack?"

"Oh, I just don't——" Lori stopped. Then she said, "I didn't really think about it. I just knew Jack didn't do it."

I was standing there, feeling numb. I'd been accused of lots of things in the old days, and usually I'd been guilty, if not of that particular thing, then of something else.

"How do you know I didn't do it?" I said.

"Cut it out!" Lori flared. "You've got to stand up for yourself now, not go around like a whipped dog!"

"You really do, you know." Jake was more gentle. "I

mean you've got to keep your head up, man. You're an innocent guy and you're being framed and you've got to think about that and *act* like that.''

It was funny in a way. They believed I was innocent, all right, but they were afraid I didn't know how to act innocent. And maybe they were right.

The bell rang. Kids came trickling into homeroom. I stood there for a minute, looking back and forth from Lori to Jake, not knowing what to say. Finally I just grinned, trying to tell them thanks, and went to my seat.

Then our homeroom teacher came in. Her name was Mrs. Cable. Since I didn't have her for any classes, I didn't know her very well. She had short gray hair and a pleasant kind of motherly face. First she took the roll and then she looked down at her clipboard and said, ''Jack Delaney, would you report to the principal's office, please?''

Would I? Sure. I nodded to her, but she was looking at her clipboard. I felt strange. But it wasn't a new feeling. In the old days I'd been sent to the principal's office plenty of times, and then later at Marshfield to the deputy's office more than once.

I got up and walked to the back of the room and out the door. Fifty people must have been looking at me, but I didn't see them. It's something you learn, or your body learns, after you've been in trouble enough times. You don't catch anybody's eye. You just move along through the people and keep to yourself.

I walked down the hall and around a turn and right into the principal's office. Or, rather, the main outer office. Two women were standing behind the long counter. I didn't know either of them.

''I'm Jack Delaney,'' I said.

''Oh, yes!'' one of them answered, like it was a pleasant surprise. ''You can go right in, Jack.'' She pointed to a door. I had to go around the counter, through a little swinging gate. I'd been here before, when I registered. The door had RONALD LANE, PRINCIPAL painted on it in gold letters. I knocked.

"Come in," a voice called.

I went in and saw Mr. Lane standing behind his desk. Somebody else was in the office, too, sitting off to the side. I didn't look at that somebody else.

"You wanted to see me?"

"Sit down, Jack." He indicated a chair in front of his desk. Mr. Lane was brusque, but that was his style. He was always brusque, always in a hurry to do three other things. Now he sat down, leaned back in his swivel chair, and studied me for a moment without saying anything. For once he didn't seem to be in a hurry.

"Do you know why you're here?"

"I got an idea."

"Yes, well——" He stopped, shook his head. He was pretty young to be a principal, I'd always thought. Not much over thirty, with sort of a businessman's face, if that makes any sense. "I know this is unpleasant for you," he said, "and it's unpleasant for me. But the first thing I want you to understand is that we're not jumping to any conclusions."

"About what?" I knew I was being a wiseass; it was like an old habit coming back.

Mr. Lane frowned. "Actually, Jack, this matter is already out of my hands. I presume you know what I'm talking about—the break-in over the weekend."

"I just heard about it." The wiseass routine was no good. I'd try to play this as straight as I could.

"Well, it's not a matter the school can handle internally. Breaking and entering is a felony. We had no choice but to turn the matter over to the police."

I kept my eyes on the principal. The other man in the room, sitting against the far wall, over on my right . . . that would be the police, no doubt. I knew he was there, but I didn't want to look at him. I knew it was stupid. I couldn't make him go away by not looking at him.

"This is Police Chief Williams," Mr. Lane said, turning toward that other figure in the room. "He'd like to ask you a few questions."

So it was time. I had to look at him. The man. For a long time I had been sure I'd never again have to look at the man from the kind of place I was sitting in right now. But it was time again, so I gave him a good look while I was at it. He had gray hair, cut long, combed back in an old-fashioned way, thick gray mustache, long stern face, and wide-open brown eyes that didn't seem to fit the rest of him.

He stood up and stuck out his hand. I stood up, too, and we shook. Very formal and weird. He was a big old man, about six-four and no fat. Not so old, either, I realized. He didn't try to impress with his grip, but his hand felt strong.

"Corwin Williams," he said, voice deep and slow and easy.

"*You're* Corwin Williams?"

He nodded, looking at me, watchful and serious.

I sat down again, still staring at him. How come things always came round and tied knots like this? It didn't make any sense that Corwin Williams would turn out to be the man. But why did it have to make sense? I had been holding myself tight all the way from homeroom to this instant . . . and now I lost the hold. Everything was suddenly swirling out of control. Uncle Fred and my aunt . . . Cindy Farr . . . Coach Foss . . . Benny and the guys . . . what were they all going to think?

"Is this your hat?" He held it out—a brown leather cap, round, with a very short bill.

"Yeah." I swallowed. "Yes, sir. I mean, it looks like it."

"I want you to be sure." He handed me the cap.

"It's mine."

"When was the last time you wore it?"

"I don't know. Week or so ago. I lost it."

"Where'd you lose it?"

"I'm not sure. I thought I had it with me in the locker room one day. But maybe I didn't. Maybe I left it somewhere else. I just don't know."

"Do you know where we found it?"

"I heard."

"No idea how it could have gotten there?"

"No, I don't. All I know is I didn't leave it there."

"Think you can beat Columbus-Murdock this year?"

"I don't know. I never played against them."

"You got any idea who might have left your cap at the scene of this burglary?"

I shook my head. He was a gray fox, this Corwin Williams.

He leaned back in his chair and touched his nose with a long knobby forefinger. "If somebody left your cap there, that would be an attempt at a frame-up. Now who would try to frame you for a job like this. And why?"

"I'm telling you I don't know, but somebody did. That's for sure."

"You're telling me you don't know, but if you'll pardon my saying so, I can't quite swallow that. Man usually knows who his enemies are."

"Look, it's no secret, I probably got at least a dozen enemies in this school. I mean since the team split up. But I can't say I think a certain guy did it. Didn't you find any fingerprints?"

"No prints. Not even on your hat."

I didn't quite get it until he went on.

"Leather doesn't take prints well, but there weren't even any smudges. Does seem a little strange you'd wipe your own hat clean." The gray-haired police chief stared moodily at my leather cap. With his head bent like that, and the silver hair combed back and falling loose and curly down his neck behind his ears, he suddenly reminded me of Buffalo Bill. It was a nutty thought. But I've noticed that when you're in trouble, you sometimes get nutty thoughts. Maybe it helps keep you sane. Or crazy. But at least alive.

"I'll have to hold this hat for a while," he said. "It's the only evidence we've got."

"So you still think I did it?"

He frowned up at the ceiling, then directed his slightly pop-eyed gaze at Mr. Lane, who had been sitting behind his desk very quietly ever since he turned me over to the chief of police. "What do you think, Ronald? Do you think Jack did it?"

"Oh, I couldn't make any comment on that." The principal immediately grabbed some papers and started shuffling them. "You shouldn't ask me a question like that, Corwin. Especially not in front of the defendant."

"He's not the defendant." Buffalo Bill waved one of his big hands. "He's a suspect. That's all."

"Yes, I know, but——" Mr. Lane shook his head. "This is now a police matter, and Jack has certain rights." He stopped and gave the chief a frown. "You haven't informed him of his rights. Have you?"

Buffalo Bill let his jaw drop a notch. "This boy is not under arrest. We're just talking about his hat. That's all."

Mr. Lane reddened. I got a kick out of it, the easy way the old man put him down. There was something going on here, too. Between the two of them. And I wasn't sure what it was.

"Well, this is kind of a mess, Jack," the chief said, putting my cap on his knee, frowning at it. "We've got a burglary here and we've got your hat and we've got a possible frame-up. I don't know what the hell it means. What I do know is I'm not going to arrest you, not without more proof than this wiped-clean hat."

I didn't know what to say. I was grateful to him in a

way, and I guess I respected him, but I still didn't like the place I was in.

"You can go," Corwin Williams said, shooting me what seemed like a friendly glance. "Unless the principal wants you to stay."

"No, no, that's perfectly all right," Mr. Lane said. He didn't shoot me any kind of a glance.

As I put my hand on the doorknob, Corwin Williams said, "Oh, one more thing, Jack. Where were you on Saturday night, from about eight o'clock on?"

"I was home, with my aunt and uncle."

"No parties?"

"No. I was home all night. Oh, wait a minute!" I remembered and wished I had something else to remember. "Did this happen on Saturday night?"

"Looks like it. The custodian discovered the break-in at eight Sunday morning, when he made his regular check."

"Well, look. I went out for a walk Saturday night. I'd forgotten for a minute. But I did go for a walk, around nine-thirty or ten."

"Do you often go for walks alone at night?"

"Yeah, sometimes. I get bored watchin' the tube and—I don't know—just restless, I guess."

"Haven't you got a girl friend?" He seemed genuinely concerned, like a counselor or something.

"Not exactly."

"My God, things must've changed more than I thought. In my day a high school football star used to have to beat the girls off with a club."

"I guess times have changed."

"Nah, not that much. You're probably just shy, Jack."

What the hell kind of a police chief was this?

"Go back to your classes. But just for the record—no just for my own satisfaction—I'm going to ask you straight out, one time: Did you break into this school?"

"No."

"Okay, forget about it. Start thinking about Murdock. They'll be tough, so don't say I didn't warn you."

I got out of that office and through the outer office, which was starting to fill up with teachers and students. In the hall I hesitated for a minute, looked for a clock. It was almost the end of the period. I had science next. Much as I liked Mrs. Swanson, I didn't feel like going to science. I didn't feel like talking to anybody or listening to anybody. But what else could I do? If I went home this time of morning, Aunt Frieda would get very nervous. I'd have to tell them both about the whole thing tonight, anyway, and that would be soon enough.

So, I hung around in the hall till the bell rang, and then went to science. I kept pretty much to myself, which probably wasn't that unusual either, come to think of it. Some of the kids said hello, and some didn't. Actually nobody seemed to be paying much attention. But I didn't trust that. I already knew how these kids could put on that old poker face and pretend they didn't know anything. You could bet ten-to-one right now that everybody in school knew about the burglary and about my cap and about my little session with the chief of police. So why all this phony-baloney innocence? That was one thing about Marshfield. When you were in trouble down there, everybody knew and talked about it, right to your face. Either to make you feel better or feel worse, but it was up front, and that's what I liked.

That's the way it went all day. Except for a very few people. Benny caught me in the hall. "Don't worry about it, Jack. Nobody with a brain in his head thinks you had anything to do with it.''

That made me feel good for a minute. And then Jake gave me a high-sign when he saw me. And there were a couple of others. But mostly everybody just ignored the whole thing. I knew kids were talking among themselves about the break-in, but nobody was talking to me about it.

Just one teacher. Sure, Joe Foss. I met him in the hall between classes, and he called me into an empty room. When we were alone, he gave me that straight look of his and scratched his head for a minute and said, "This is a bad thing, Jack. I wish to hell it hadn't happened. All I can tell you is to hang in there. They'll get the punks who did it. Don't worry."

I didn't say anything.

"Now, look! Don't let this get you down. Nobody thinks you'd be stupid enough to leave your hat at the scene of a robbery. Then he shook his head. "Boy, there I go again! I didn't mean it that way, you know that." He grinned and gave me a punch on the shoulder. "See you at practice."

I didn't feel like going to practice, either, but I did. Keep the routine of the day going, that was all I could hang onto. Trouble was, I kept thinking about Cindy Farr all the time. Not that I thought she wouldn't believe me, but I didn't want to even have to talk to her about it. Burglary and stealing money—they were cheap messy things. I didn't want them to enter into what was starting to happen between me and Cindy.

The fact was that ordinary, respectable people don't get suspected of burglary, and nobody tries to frame them by planting their hats at the scene of the crime. All of a sudden, the whole thing between me and Cindy started to look impossible. I'd always be the guy the cops came looking for when there was a robbery in the neighborhood.

And Cindy was the classy girl who went to the private school. Her folks must be rich. What would they think when they found out their daughter's boyfriend was an ex-con? I knew what they'd think. And what they'd do, too. Shut the door in my face, that's what they'd do.

So that's the way I was feeling when I went to practice, and naturally practice didn't turn out to be too great. The other guys were nice, most of them, but I was thinking more about my aunt and uncle and about Cindy and about that gray fox Corwin Williams, and I couldn't keep my mind on football. As soon as it was over, I grabbed a quick shower and got out of the locker room fast, so I wouldn't have to talk to anybody.

I jogged all the way home. Felt as though I had a whole lot of energy inside me that I couldn't use up. As soon as I entered the kitchen and caught a glimpse of Aunt Frieda's face, I knew she had heard. She gave me a bright nervous smile and put a big plate of chocolate chip cookies on the table. I could see that she was ready to pretend that nothing had happened.

For a minute it made me angry and sort of disgusted. But that's the way people *are,* I told myself. They don't like to talk about unpleasant things. It's not their fault. Lay back now, for God's sake, and give her a chance.

And I did. I ate a couple of cookies and drank some milk and listened to my aunt talk about the weather and how she'd read in the paper it was going to be a hard winter. She was too nervous, though. I knew we couldn't keep going this way. I said, "Listen, Aunt Frieda. I know you must have heard about the break-in at school. For right now, I just want to tell you I didn't do it. When Uncle Fred comes home, I'll tell you both the whole story. Is that okay?"

She gave me a full look for the first time. "I never had the slightest doubt about that, Jack. But I've been so worried——" She stopped, with a sharp "tch-tch-tch" at herself. "No, you're right! We'll wait till Fred gets home and then just go through it once and let that be it. Now eat your cookies while I make another cup of coffee."

She was okay, Aunt Frieda was. A worrier, but she could roll with the punches, too. And once she made up her mind about something, she stuck with it.

Of course, when my uncle Fred came home the whole atmosphere changed. Aunt Frieda had supper on the table and he sat right down to it, but you could feel the anger coming out of him, the way he grabbed his fork and cut through a hamburger patty like he was killing a whole cow. I didn't feel hungry at all. I just waited, not watching him, till he'd swallowed a couple of mouthfuls.

Then he laid down his fork and said, "Now what the hell is going on, boy. Can you tell me?"

"Look, I didn't have anything to do with that break-in." I was trying to be cool, but I could hear a little quiver or quaver in my voice.

"Oh, hell, boy, I know you didn't!" He was looking at me with his eyebrows up and his eyes wide open. "I *know* you didn't. That's not what I'm talking about. But somebody left your *hat* there! Somebody's tryin' to frame you for this thing! That's what I'm talkin' about!"

I mean he was sizzling. He was so mad he was sputtering. His owly eyes kept shooting back and forth from me to Aunt Frieda. "Corwin Williams won't tell me a damn thing! Nobody *knows* a damn thing! Except that they found your hat there. I mean this is a goddam *shame*, Jack!"

And, you know, all I felt like doing was crying. I knew now I'd been afraid of how he was going to take it. Afraid he'd be suspicious and grunty, the way people are when they're pretending they believe you, but want you to know they don't really believe you, either.

It took a long time to tell my story, because Uncle Fred kept breaking in, cussing Mr. Lane and Corwin Williams and practically everybody else in Holbrook. Aunt Frieda finally told him politely but firmly to shut his big mouth and let me finish my story, which he did, with smoke still coming out of his ears.

When I finished there was a short silence except for Aunt Frieda "tch-tching" to herself. Then Uncle Fred pointed his finger at me and he moved it up and down a few times, like he was having a hard time getting it cocked.

"You know who did that, don't you?" he said. "You know as well as I do who did it!"

"No, I don't. I don't have any proof. If I did——" I stopped and thought about what I'd do if I did. "I don't even know what I'd do if I did."

"Why d'ya think Ronnie Lane was pussyfooting around that way!"

"I don't know."

"Because it's so damn obvious, that's why. It's staring him right in the face and he's scared. They're all scared. Scared to name a name."

"Well, there's no proof."

"There might be, if they'd go after it while the clues and everything are still fresh. I told Corwin Williams right to his face he ought to get hold of Wilbur Gilliam's boy and talk to him same as he did to you. And you know what he said?"

"Wilbur's boy? Do you think he did it?" Aunt Frieda was flabbergasted. "Why would he do a thing like that?"

"You know what he said?" Uncle Fred was driving straight ahead. "He said if he questioned the Gilliam boy, he'd have to question every boy in the school. And—and the girls, too." He was stuttering, now, trying to get it all out. "He said there wasn't the slightest evidence pointing at the Gilliam boy. Now how do you like that!"

"But why would *he* do it?" Aunt Frieda was stuck. "He certainly doesn't need the money."

Uncle Fred gave her a look that would have withered

the needles off a pine tree. "Jack's hat, Frieda. For God's sake! He left Jack's hat there. Because he doesn't *like* Jack. He's jealous of Jack. Can't you understand two and two!"

"I can understand two and two, all right," she snapped. "But I can't understand this. Just because he and Jack don't get along . . . that doesn't mean he *did* it. My goodness, Fred, let's try to be fair!"

It went on and on while the hamburgers got cold and the lettuce wilted. I hated to see my aunt and uncle arguing like this. They both had some right on their side, but the trouble was, the argument wasn't really about that. It was about . . . other things . . . all kinds of long-ago and never-said things.

My uncle realized it, too, because he suddenly stopped arguing and ate the rest of his supper. Not until I was helping Aunt Frieda clear the table did he speak again: "The hell of it is, Jack," he said in a low-key, matter-of-fact way, "this thing may never get solved. What you gotta do is take it in stride, best you can. You know that, don't you?"

"Yeah, I know."

"You just go to school and play football and let 'em think what they want. Your friends'll stand by you. You can count on that. And don't worry about what the rest of 'em think, or even what they say. You think you can do that?"

"I guess so."

"You *gotta* do it. You can't let this thing mess you up!"

"Your uncle is right, you know," Aunt Frieda said. "You have to protect your own life, Jack. This will pass—everything passes—but you'll still be here on this earth and you have to take care of *yourself*. As long as you know you're doing right, that's all that really counts." She smiled her trembling little smile. "I know that sounds like a Sunday school lesson, but it's absolutely true."

"I know," I said, and then I looked at her. "But taking care of yourself . . . and at the same time doing what you think is right . . . those two things don't always seem to be the same."

"No, they don't. Do they? They don't always *seem* to be the same. I had a lot of trouble with that when I was young, and still do, I'm afraid. Would you like to hear one of the things I go back to sometimes when I get confused?"

"Sure."

She got up from the table and went into the living room and came back, holding an old faded green book. "This is Ralph Waldo Emerson," she said, sitting down and giving me a nervous little smile. "I don't think he's very popular these days, but he should be. At least I think he should be." She opened the book, hunted for her place, found it, cleared her throat, wiggled to settle herself in her chair. I almost grinned, all the getting ready she had to go through. Maybe she sensed it. "Mr. Emerson is important to me," she said. "This is from an essay called 'Compensation.' Now listen." And she began to read:

The dice of God are always loaded. The world looks like a multiplication table, or a mathematical equation, which, turn it how you will, balances itself. Take what figure you will, its exact value, nor more nor less, still returns to you. Every secret is told, every crime is punished, every virtue rewarded, every wrong redressed, in silence and certainty.

"What do you think of that?" she said, looking at me sideways.

"Well, to tell you the truth, Aunt Frieda, it sounds a little too pat. Do you really believe it?"

"I believe it the way Emerson meant it," she said. "I'd

have to read you the whole essay to make it come together right. Maybe you'll read it yourself sometime?''

''Yeah, I will,'' I said. Thinking, I probably won't.

''Let me read another little piece.'' She bent to the book again. ''Listen.'' She read:

All infractions of love and equity in our social relations are speedily punished. They are punished by fear. Whilst I stand in simple relations to my fellow man, I have no displeasure in meeting him. We meet as water meets water, or as two currents of air mix, with perfect diffusion and interpenetration of nature. But as soon as there is any departure from simplicity and attempt at halfness, or good for me that is not good for him, my neighbor feels the wrong; he shrinks from me as far as I have shrunk from him; his eyes no longer seek mine; there is war between us; there is hate in him and fear in me.

She closed the book, and you could tell, the way her hands touched it, how she felt about it. ''You see, he doesn't say you get paid back directly, in the same kind, or even always promptly. But he says that in the end everything balances. And I believe him. And not just him . . . I believe what my life has taught me.''

''It's no use preaching that stuff, Frieda,'' my uncle said, coming into the room and standing by the table, looking down at my aunt, but fondly. ''People don't believe it anymore.''

''I'm not preaching,'' she said. ''And people do believe it, whether they know it or not.''

''Well, I don't know.'' He looked at me. ''What do you think, Jack?''

''I don't know, either,'' I said. ''But I guess I couldn't say for sure that I don't believe it.''

95

That's where we left it, and I don't know how much it meant to me or if it did me any good, but it was something to think about during the next days.

I went to school and I went to practice, and though I tried to be cool and tried to remember all the things I was supposed to remember, it was still a hard trip. People were treating me differently from the way they had a week ago. I wasn't imagining it Some of the kids were even friendlier in a funny way. I guess those were the ones who thought there was something romantic about being a thief. I already knew that was all baloney. Some thieves in the movies may seem romantic, but everything I'd seen in real life had shown me it was a dirty business. Thieves are always worried, always running scared. I couldn't tell these kids that. And didn't even want to.

Several times I passed Peanuts Gilliam in the halls. Though we didn't have any classes together, the school wasn't so big that two people could stay entirely out of each other's way unless they really worked at it.

The first time we met he gave me a sharp glance, then looked away. The next time I got more of a puzzled look from him. Maybe he was expecting me to jump him or challenge him somehow.

Most of the other kids and teachers were polite enough, but a distance had opened up, even with the guys on the team. No matter how hard they tried to be friendly, there was always a little something else poking its head up. Except in a very few cases—Jake and Benny and, yes, Lori Curtin Those three were steady as rocks. Jeff Wagner was okay, too. And Coach Foss, he was really good. He didn't talk any more about the frame-up part of it, but he let me know he didn't have any doubts. And why was that so important? I kept telling myself I didn't care what people thought—and knew it was a big lie—because if I really didn't care, then good opinions wouldn't matter to me any more than bad ones. I started to understand how we are all, all the time, kidding ourselves about our egos.

On Wednesday I got a big surprise and didn't really know how to handle it. Lori Curtin caught up with me in the hall, as she often did these days, and asked me straight out for a date. I mean that's what it amounted to. Here's what she said: "Hey, Jack, my father's going to let me have his car this Saturday night. How would you like to take me to a drive-in movie?"

"What?"

"A drive-in. You've heard of them." She was giving me that slanty look. "Over near Millersville. They're showing *King Kong*. I've never seen it, and this might be my last chance."

A vision of Cindy Farr flashed through my mind. She had already sent word through Linda that she might not be able to make it again this weekend. Two weekends in a row, and all of a sudden Cindy Farr seemed very far away. Besides, I didn't feel like going to another one of Linda's parties, not for a while, anyway. And I had a sneaking lousy hunch that Cindy might have heard about the burglary and was embarrassed or something to see me right now.

"Well, all right. You know, you're the first person who ever asked me to go to the movies."

"I'm not *exactly* asking you to go to the movies. That'd mean I'd have to pay your way."

"Oh, I thought that was what you meant."

"Okay, I'll pay your way." She was smiling up at me, her gaze not so slanty now.

"You'll have to drive. I don't have a license."

"I wouldn't expect you to have a license, Jackson. You're the world's greatest football player and maybe the world's nicest guy, but sometimes I'm not so sure you should be allowed out of the house by yourself."

With that, she ducked into her English class. I stared after her, wondering what she meant. Was I such a goof?

No, I wasn't a goof. I was just dumb about some things, that's all. It hit me right then that in a certain real way I wasn't anywhere near as old as the rest of these Holbrook seniors. Those years in Marshfield, where I grew up physically, didn't count as real-world years. In those years I never talked to a girl, never talked with real freedom and honesty to *anybody*. So now the physical part of me was eighteen years old, but the rest of me . . . well, I didn't know how old the rest of me was, but sometimes it sure felt like fourteen.

On Thursday I managed to catch Coach Foss alone for a minute during practice. I told him I didn't think I should play in Saturday's game.

"Come off it, Jack! That's the worst possible thing you could do!"

I shook my head. "I've been thinkin' about it. I'll be like a sideshow freak out there. And half the people in town'll be saying I shouldn't be playing for the school while I'm still under suspicion for burglary."

"Jack, most of the people in this town don't give a damn about that burglary. And they don't give a damn about you. They wouldn't give a damn if the First National Bank got blown up, as long as they got their money back."

A couple of other players were trotting toward us. Foss waved them away. Then he started digging into the top of his head with his fingernails.

"You mean I'm making myself too important."

"No, not too important. But the world is going right on. And what you have to do is forget about this damn burglary and climb back aboard. If you don't play Saturday, you'll be letting the train move along without you."

I wasn't positive I got the message right. But I said, okay, I'd play. It was lesson number two, or maybe number ten. The lessons were piling up and I didn't even know if I was learning them.

And then on Saturday, as we were dressing for the

game, Benny Younger told me that Cindy Farr had called Linda and said she'd be able to make it after all. "And she said she hoped you'd be there."

"Where?"

"At Linda's. She's having another party. Didn't she tell you?"

"Yeah, I guess she did."

"I'll pick you up about eight."

"Benny, I can't go."

"Why not! I just told you Cindy'll be there, man."

"I just can't make it, Benny. You tell her . . . no, don't tell her anything. I'll have to tell her."

"Tell her what?" Benny was staring at me. "Look, Jack, it's your life. But Cindy Farr, I don't have to tell you, is some kind of a girl. And she likes you, man. If you like her . . . well, don't go do something stupid."

I couldn't talk anymore. "Tell her I'll call her." I managed to croak the words out. And then I turned away and honest-to-God didn't know anything till the game was over and guys were clapping me on the shoulder and trying to hug me. I felt like I was waking up from a doze. And the game was the memory of a dream. I knew we'd won, big. And I knew I'd covered a lot of ground. But it was all very hazy and disconnected.

After showers, Benny came by again. "You won't change your mind?"

"I can't, Benny. I gave my word on something else, and I can't back out."

"Well, you could. I mean you can do whatever you want to do."

I shook my head. "I can't."

"Okay. I'll give her your message." He lifted his hand. "Hell of a game, Jack. I never saw anybody play football like that before."

Then Jake came over. "You all right, Jack?"

"Sure. Why?"

"I don't know, man. But the way you were playing today . . . if I didn't know you better I'd have thought you had overdosed on speed." He was eyeing me . . . very curious, and maybe a bit cautious. "Tell me the truth, Jack." He lowered his voice. "Do you remember anything about that game?"

I hated to admit it. "Not a hell of a lot." It made me sound like I was going nuts.

"That's what I thought. Listen, man. You were playing like a guided missile. But that's no good. You'll kill yourself. Plus scare everybody else to death."

I was putting on my jacket.

"You walking home?"

"Yeah."

"I'll walk along with you a ways. Cut down Forester. It's just as close."

He'd never done it before. But I was in no mood to question. I just felt glad to have his company.

"You sure you're all right?" he said as we walked across the big parking lot.

"Course, I'm all right." But I was shivering and trying to hunker down inside a jacket that wasn't quite big enough for me. "Cold night for October, hey?"

"I'm worried about you, man."

"What're you talking about?"

"You gotta get easy with yourself, Jack. Or you're gonna flip out."

"Come on!"

"I've seen it in the ghetto. A dude gets tighter and tighter and tighter and tighter, till he hums like a violin string when you touch him. That's the way you been going all week. You can't keep tightening up, man. There's a limit. I've seen dudes go flying out of their heads—something like you did in the game today—only they maybe had a knife in their hands, and when it was over they didn't remember nothin'. Nothin'. Just like you."

100

"Are you serious?"

"Serious, man."

We had stopped under the streetlight at Forester. I looked at Jake. His dark-brown face was serious, all right.

"You gotta get out from under this load you're carrying," he said. "You don't have to prove anything. To hell with Peanuts and to hell with Holbrook and to hell with everybody, if it comes down to that. You gotta relax and just slip along easy for a while. And stop *worrying*. Nothing's worth that kind of worry. Dig?"

"Okay, doctor. I'll work on it." Trying to be cool. But not feeling so cool. I knew I'd been worrying about the burglary, but I hadn't known it showed that much, or at all. I had thought I was keeping everything under control, just poker-facing it through the week. What had happened in the game, though—that scared me. Maybe I *was* close to flipping out. It was a bad thing to think about. Scary. So I tried to stop thinking.

Uncle Fred was quiet at supper. We were all quiet. I should have been hungry as a horse, but I got filled up on three mouthfuls.

"Don't you feel well, Jack?" Aunt Frieda asked when she noticed I wasn't eating.

"I feel all right. I'm just not hungry. I don't know why."

"You played too hard." Uncle Fred put down his knife and fork and gave me his owlish look. "I saw the game. Me and Corwin Williams and Deke Snyder, we went together. Corwin said you were playing too hard, said you were pushing yourself too far. Said if the coach had any sense he'd have taken you out, given you a breather."

"Is that right?"

"That's right." He looked at his wife. "You shoulda seen that game, Frieda! Next time you gotta go. Jack here . . . well, I'm telling you. . . . He stopped and shook his head. "How many touchdowns did you score, Jack?"

"I don't know."

"He doesn't even know. He scored about four or five. Corwin says you're a natural, but he says you played *too* hard. Says you'll break yourself up that way."

"What makes him such an expert?"

"He used to play. He knows football, boy. You better believe it."

"Are you sure you feel all right, Jack?" Aunt Frieda was watching me with a little worried frown. "You look kind of pale."

"He played too hard," Uncle Fred said. "I just got through telling you."

"No, I'm fine," I said. "Honest."

"But you haven't eaten anything."

"Maybe I'll eat some more after I get home."

"Got a hot date?" Uncle Fred tipped me a wink.

"Nah. I'm just going to the movies with a girl."

"The one you were at the dance with?"

"No. How'd you know about her?"

"Oh, word gets around. Not many secrets in a town like Holbrook, Jack. I heard she was a very pretty girl. Very nice girl, too. But from out of town, hey?"

"Yeah, from Columbus."

"Gonna see her again?"

"That's none of your *business*, Fred!" Aunt Frieda said.

"Don't hurt none. Jack don't mind, do you, Jack?"

I shook my head.

"Gonna see her again?"

"I don't know for sure."

"Who you going out with tonight?"

"Fred!"

He ignored her. Just sat waiting with a look of good-natured curiosity. You couldn't resent a guy like my uncle Fred, even if he was nosey.

"Her name's Lori Curtin."

"Benjamin Curtin's daughter? Sure, I know who she is." He opened his mouth to go on. His eyes opened a little wider, too. But then he kind of settled in on himself and didn't say anything.

"You're worse than an old gossip!" Aunt Frieda snapped. "Don't pay any attention to him, Jack. He's just got to know everything that's going on. Every little thing."

Uncle Fred belched, pardoned himself, stared innocently at his wife.

"I'll leave this roast in the refrigerator. You help yourself when you get home. Maybe your appetite'll be back by then."

"Might be at that," Uncle Fred snorted into his coffee cup. "Nothing like a good movie to give a boy back his appetite."

12

Lori Curtin's father's car was a Chevy Impala. Conservative for a girl like Lori. She didn't drive it conservative, though. Not reckless, but fast and quick. I caught myself envying her. Probably the first time in my life I ever wished I could do something as well as a girl could.

"You're a good driver."

She turned her head, smiling. "Thanks. You're the first man who ever told me that."

"Is that right?"

"Yes, sir, Jackson, that is right." She had her eyes back on the road. It was dark, but I could see her face in the glow from the dashboard. She was still smiling. Though I knew she was making fun of me a little bit, it didn't bother me. Lori had a way about her. She didn't mock you out of meanness or what you might call competitiveness. She did it because she liked you, and you could feel that all the time.

It was only thirty miles to Millersville. We didn't talk a whole lot, and yet we were comfortable with each other. I was thinking about my other trip to Millersville, the day Peanuts and Bobby Johns and the rest of them had been kicked off the team. Was that only a month ago? This fall already seemed about three years long.

Lori took an exit off the freeway. Then a couple of turns and a couple of miles and there it was, the drive-in. Big sign. *King Kong,* sure enough.

"Oh, *hell!*" Lori said.

"What's the matter?"

"I don't know, but there's something wrong. Cars are coming out. The place is dark."

I could see it now. Confusion in the lanes leading to the ticket booths. Cars backing and turning.

"Wouldn't you know!" She was really disgusted. "Look!" We were getting closer to the gate. Now I saw the hastily lettered sign nailed to one of the ticket windows: SORRY, NO MOVIE TONIGHT. ELECTRICAL PROBLEMS.

"Electrical problems!" she jeered, ripping the Impala around in a hundred-eighty-degree turn, missing an old truck by two inches. "The one night in the year I want to see *King Kong* and they have electrical problems." She slammed the Impala into a parking space in front of the drive-in, cut the motor, and sat there for a moment, staring straight ahead at nothing. "I must be a jinx," she said. "I'm really starting to believe I'm a jinx."

"Nah, it's all right. Maybe there's another movie?"

"Not around here. Hey!" She turned toward me with new energy. "What we could do, we could go to the late show up at Denby. I forget what's playing, but we can call them and find out. Do you want to do that?"

"How far's Denby?"

"Not *far.* We'll be home by . . . do you have a curfew?"

"No, but. . . ."

"But, but, but! We'll be home by twelve-thirty, one at the latest. How's that?"

"That's fine." I felt strange, I guess, from being driven around by a girl who was doing all the thinking for both of us.

"Great!" She turned the key and the motor came back to life. "It's the first time I ever took a man to the movies, you know, and I don't want it to just fizzle out."

She put the car on the road. "There's a drive-in, I mean an eating drive-in, down here a little ways. I think they have a phone."

The drive-in was called the Chuckwagon. One of those old-fashioned local places. I guess there wasn't enough business around here for a McDonald's or a Burger King. I went with Lori to the phone booth. She put in a dime, got the number from information, put in some more coins, dialed. Talked and listened. When she came out of the booth, she was beaming.

"Have you ever seen *The Sting*?"

"No."

"Me neither. I guess it's an oldie. Robert Redford and Paul Newman. It might be fun."

"Okay." I hesitated. "Can't I pay for half the phone call?"

"Oh, God!" She laughed and took hold of my arm. "You worry too much, Jackson, you really do." She gave my arm a squeeze and laughed. "I'll tell you what. The second feature doesn't start till ten; so if you really want to spend your money, you can buy me a chocolate malt. How's that?"

"Okay."

"You get it and I'll wait for you in the car."

"Don't you want a hamburg or something, too?"

"No! I have to watch my figure." She tilted her head in one of her slanty looks, then turned, and ran toward the car. She was wearing tight jeans and a short red jacket.

You could tell she was a dancer from the way she ran.

I decided to get a cheeseburger and a root beer for myself. While I waited at the pickup counter I was thinking of the differences between Lori Curtin and Cindy Farr. They were both open and honest, at least as far as I could tell, but Lori had more confidence. She never hesitated to say what was on her mind. You knew where you stood with Lori, I was sure. With Cindy you might not. Cindy was more complicated and—the word crossed my mind—more "delicate"? In the sense of being more fragile? Yes. Cindy had to protect herself in ways that Lori didn't. Cindy was. . . . That's enough of that! I told myself, you're out with Lori now. She's right, boy. You do worry too much.

When I got back to the car Lori was listening to the radio. She had the motor running and the heater on, but I noticed she had the windows cracked, too. She wasn't careless, she was just a fast mover.

"What's that music?"

"It's reggae. You like?"

"I don't know anything about it."

"It comes from Jamaica. It's very sexy music."

I could hear how it might be. Even to an old tin ear like me.

We ate and drank for a while and listened to the radio. She wouldn't take any of my cheeseburger.

"Jack, can I ask you a personal question?"

"Sure." I looked at her. Her gaze was straight.

"How are you feeling inside? I mean really feeling."

I had just taken another big bite of cheeseburger. It gave me an excuse to chew for a minute.

"I don't mean about me," she said quickly. "I mean about yourself and, well, just everything in general."

"I feel okay. Why?" I swallowed the last of my root beer.

"Now don't get mad at me . . . but you don't act okay."

"Meaning what?" I knew what, though. "Maybe it's my natural way. Maybe I'm just weird."

"No. You're different from a couple of weeks ago. Not that you were ever all *that* relaxed, but lately you're so tense . . . and closed off . . . you make people afraid to talk to you."

"You seem to do okay."

I felt lousy. Why couldn't I tell her I felt lousy?

She took a breath and turned away. "I'm sorry I said anything."

"Oh, that's okay. I guess I have been acting a little . . . defensive, maybe. If I could just get out from under this damn burglary! Everybody lookin' at me sideways all the time."

"But they're *not*. That's the whole thing. I don't know a single living soul who thinks you did it. They all think Peanuts did it."

"So it's all in my head."

"Well . . . that doesn't mean you're paranoid or any-thing. It's probably natural for you to feel that way."

"Probably." I gave a snort of anger or self-disgust or something. "Boy, I feel like a jerk."

"Well, don't. It's just that Peanuts, if he did it, or whoever did it picked the perfect and, I mean, the cruelest way to try to hurt you."

"You think maybe Peanuts didn't do it?"

"Oh, I don't know. What I do know is that you've only seen one side of him. He's not as rotten as you think he is, or as the rest of them think he is, either."

"You sound like my aunt Frieda."

"I know it sounds goofy." She was picking at her fingernails. "But under that big tough-guy front of his . . ."

· He's just a lost little boy."

"You're not so far wrong, you know.'

"Aaah. . . ." I could feel pressure boiling inside me. "I don't even *know* the guy. And all he's done is mess with me ever since I got here. I think he's a psycho."

"He acts like one sometimes," she agreed. "But I think it's just that you've got him all messed up inside and . . . ."

"I got *him* all messed up!"

"And he's got you all messed up," she went on calmly, "and neither one of you knows what's happening."

"You know, you were making sense a minute ago, but I can't buy this baloney."

"Will you listen to me for a minute and then decide if it's baloney?"

"Okay."

"Peanuts is jealous of you. Envious. And not just because you're a better football player. It's a lot more complicated than that. You see, Peanuts made a place for himself in Holbrook by being tougher than anybody else. He didn't come here to school until eighth grade—he'd been in private schools and a military school. Nobody liked him at first. We all thought he was just a rich spoiled brat. So he set out to show us different. If Bobby Johns broke three windows, Peanuts would break six. Every time there was a fight between two boys, Peanuts would challenge the winner. And he'd usually beat him. He didn't care how big he was."

"So he's the Holbrook super-stud. So what?"

"So he set himself up to be that. He set himself up to be the baddest guy around. And after a while he started to believe it.

"But then you came to town. And this is what you have to understand . . . you have to try to see it from inside Peanuts's head. He's pretending to be bad, but when he sees you, he sees somebody who really *is* bad."

I tried to interrupt.

She shushed me. "Wait. I mean it's the way *Peanuts* sees things. You've actually been in jail. You came off the streets. You're quiet, but there's a look about you that says, Don't push. You let the air out of Peanuts's balloon by just walking into the school. Do you understand what I'm trying to say."

"Some of it. You sound like a psychology professor."

She laughed. "Don't tell anybody, but that's what I want to be."

"Then you might know the rules are different out here. I mean the way people think and act, I can't seem to get hold of it."

"Maybe it's because there aren't as many rules," Lori said slowly. "Or they're more flexible—I don't know—something like that."

"More than that." I was starting to see it. Vaguely, and maybe I couldn't explain it, but all of a sudden I was starting to get a true feeling of where my troubles lay. "There are probably *more* rules out here," I said, "only most of them aren't written down. I get in trouble because I want everything to be set."

"You've got to give yourself time," Lori said, her voice so low I could hardly hear it. "God, you've only been out a few months. I think you're doing just great."

"What I've been doing is letting somebody mess up my life while I just sat there. I haven't even tried to understand it or do anything about it."

"Well. . . ." She swallowed. "Sometimes you have to wait till things become clear."

"Yeah, but my waitin' time is done." I could feel something good happening to me. Like a safety valve had popped in the top of my skull. All that extra steam was whistling out, leaving just the right amount to run my engine the way it was supposed to run.

"What are you going to do?"

109

"Peanuts tried to frame me. I'm not going to let him get away with it."

"But you can't prove it!"

"I think I can."

"How?"

"I'm gonna ask him."

She stared at me in blank amazement. Then she started to nod her head, little short sharp nods. "Absolutely! Why didn't I think of that?"

"What time is it?"

She looked at her watch. "Quarter to nine."

"Any idea where Peanuts would be on a Saturday night?"

"Oh-oh. You mean you want to see him right now?"

"I'd like to."

"Well, he's probably at Harley's. It's a drive-in west of Holbrook. He'll be drinking beer and listening to his retainers tell him how bad he is. That's his idea of a really big Saturday night."

"You sound bitter."

"Oh, I suppose I am." She handed me her malt cup. "Will you throw this in the trash can for me?"

I got rid of our garbage and climbed back in the car beside her. "I used to have some hopes for Peanuts," she said quietly. "I mean I thought he might outgrow all that macho silliness."

"You still think he's a good guy underneath?"

"I really don't know." She seemed to have lost a lot of her energy. She put the car in gear and headed for Holbrook. The radio was playing soft music for a change. I guess neither one of us felt like talking.

Then as we left the freeway, she said, "I knew I was jinxed. Can't get a man to go to the movies with me even when I pay his way." But she was smiling again, and I knew things were okay.

"We'll go next week."

"Sure we will." She wheeled the big Chevy down Holbrook's main street and right out the other side of town. "There's one thing, Jack," she said, as the lights of Harley's appeared down the road. "I think Peanuts will tell you the truth—it'd be a point of honor with him. But he might want to fight you, too. Have you thought about that?"

"Yeah."

"I don't want you to get hurt."

"I don't either."

She reached over and patted my knee. It made me feel good. Not sexy, but almost grown up for a change, like we were two people who understood each other and didn't have to put up any fronts.

13

"There's his car!" She passed the blue Audi. Several guys were standing around it, one leaning on the door with his head in the window.

Lori found a parking place a few cars down. I said, "I'll see you in a few minutes," and started to get out. She put her hand on my shoulder and when I turned, her face was right there, an inch away. She kissed me or I kissed her. I don't know. We kissed each other.

"For luck," she said, and smiled. I didn't say anything. She was only the second girl I had kissed in four years.

Walking toward Peanuts's car, my body felt stiff, maybe from the game that afternoon, maybe from sitting still too long. When I got to his car I went around to the driver's side. These guys were standing there, but I didn't even see who they were. Peanuts was sitting behind the wheel, with the window open. He looked up at me and didn't even blink.

"Hey, hotshot! What're you doin' in this neck of the woods?"

"I want to talk to you a minute. Could we do it in private?"

He hesitated for a fraction of a second, then said, "Sure," opened the door, and climbed out. "Want a beer?"

"No, thanks."

He was carrying a can of beer. "Come on, we'll go around back." As he started toward the rear of the drive-in, he turned and said, "You guys stay here." The rest of the way we walked in silence, Peanuts taking an occasional swig from his beer can. I could feel him looking at me once or twice, but I didn't want to start talking till we had stopped and were face to face.

The area behind Harley's was a mess—huge garbage containers and piles of boxes and all kinds of junk. Peanuts stopped in a clear space.

"Well, what's on your mind?" He was standing unconcerned, and though the light was dim, I could see he was watching me pretty close.

"Did you set me up on that school break-in?"

"Come again?"

"Hey, don't play cute. I want to know if you broke into school and left my cap there."

"You gotta be kiddin'!"

"No, I'm not kiddin'."

"Well, for Christ sake! You didn't do it? You know, I never could figure you breaking into that school."

"I'm asking you if *you* did it!"

"Of course, I didn't do it. What kind of an asshole do you think I am!"

"I don't know what kind."

112

Peanuts looked at me for a second. I thought he was going to start swinging. But he didn't. He said, "Why didn't you say something before?"

"I don't know. I wasn't thinking straight."

"Well, for Christ sake," he said again. "You know, when you came to my car, I thought you wanted to fight." He tossed the beer can over his shoulder. "It ain't littering, not in a dump like this."

"If you didn't do it, who did?"

"How the hell do I know who did it?" He was peering at me, and for an instant I wondered if maybe he didn't believe me. Just like maybe I didn't believe him. But the funny thing was, I did believe him.

"Hey." He said it almost to himself. "I guess I do know who did it." He looked startled, as though somebody had flashed a light in his eyes. "Gotta be."

"Who?"

"You wait here, will ya? I'll only be a minute."

I said okay. He took off on a run, and was back in not much over a minute. He wasn't alone this time. Two shadowy figures moved toward me across Harley's backyard. Was this another setup? For a second I thought of running. Nobody can fight two guys at once . . . unless he's in the movies. I looked around for some help. A pool cue would even it up a little. But there wasn't a pool cue in sight.

"Hey, Delaney!" Peanuts's voice was hoarse and urgent. "Cool it, man! This is truce time." Coming closer, he said, "I should've told you I was bringing somebody."

I looked at the other guy. It was Bobby Johns. That didn't exactly ease my mind, either.

"So . . . this is it," Peanuts said, drawing it out. He should have been an actor, I was thinking, the way he liked to set the stage for his big appearances.

"This is what?" Bobby Johns said, and his voice, too loud, gave it all away.

"You busted into the school, didn't ya?" Peanuts said.

"Are you nuts?"

"And you left Delaney's hat there, didn't ya?"

Johns looked all around the yard, then back at his questioner. "What're you trying to do, Peanuts?"

Peanuts jabbed a finger at him. "You better tell me the truth."

"I ain't telling you nothin'! Specially not with him standing there."

"You know, Bobby, if this was a TV story, right now's when I'd bust you one in the jaw."

Johns was staring at him unbelievingly. "I don't dig this," he said. "I don't dig any part of this."

"All right," Peanuts said, letting out his breath in what could have been a sigh. "I know it's all fouled up." He had his head down, his blond hair falling over his eyes. "Thing is, I got nothing against anybody for robbing that school. But trying to frame somebody else for the job— that's what I don't go for."

"What's the big deal?" Bobby Johns had gained a little courage. "Whoever did it. You were trying to get this guy yourself. So maybe somebody helped you out. What're you getting so holy about?"

"It's not that I'm getting holy, Bobby," Peanuts said earnestly. "It's just that whoever pulled this job never stopped to think that Delaney would automatically blame me for it. And that he might convince a lot of other people that I did it, too. I mean, it puts me in a bad light."

"Oh, geez, I guess nobody ever thought about that."

Peanuts nodded and raised his head. He was grinning. "Forget it. I can handle it." He gave Bobby a whack on the back. "You did do it, didn't ya?"

"Sure I did it. But I never meant to get you involved, Peanuts." He looked over at me. "I don't care if this jerk hears it. If he says anything, I'll just deny it. Who's gonna believe him, anyway?"

"Me," Peanuts said, still grinning.

"*You*?" Bobby Johns looked stunned. Then intelligence flickered back into his eyes. "Why, you son of a bitch!" He started to turn, I guess, to run away. Peanuts hit him once, just in front of the ear. A long hard punch that knocked Bobby completely off his feet.

"What do you want to do with him?" Peanuts asked. Bobby was lying on the ground, not moving.

"I don't know." Everything had switched ends too fast. "I thought he was your friend."

"He is."

This Peanuts Gilliam was something else. But what was he? A real psycho? Or just a devious bastard who was playing his own game? Or was he, possibly, on the level?

Bobby got up. He didn't seem hurt, except probably his feelings.

"Let's take him down to the jail," Peanuts said.

"I don't know." And I didn't. I just plain didn't know what to do.

"You want to get out from under, right?"

Bobby Johns was standing off a little to the side, looking at Peanuts and then at me.

"Yeah, but I think I need a couple of minutes to get this straightened out in my head."

"C'mon. We'll get in the car and drive around for a while. You, too, Bobby."

Bobby nodded, not exactly like a zombie, but I had a feeling that if Peanuts had told him to start walking to California, Bobby would have nodded and set off.

I found myself moving along with the two of them toward Peanuts's car. I'd gotten rid of one weight, but it looked like I'd picked up another. Suddenly I remembered Lori.

"Hey, a friend brought me out here. I better tell her to wait."

"This business may take a while," Peanuts said. "If she

wants to go home I'll drop you off—her house or yours or anywhere in between."

"How come you're gettin' so damn accommodating?"

"Beats me." He laughed.

"He's nuts, that's why," Bobby Johns said quietly.

Maybe he *is* nuts, I was thinking after I left them and was looking for Lori's car. That would explain a lot of things.

"Jack!" I turned, and here came Lori, running between cars, from the direction of Harley's backyard.

"What the hell are you doing?" This night was rapidly getting beyond me.

"I was scared," she panted, "when I saw Peanuts come and get Bobby Johns. I thought they were going to beat you up. Or maybe bury your body. So I followed them."

"No kiddin'?" I stared at her in admiration. "You got guts."

"Hiding behind a dumpster doesn't take much guts. Come on, I'm freezing!" We got into her car. She turned the motor and the heater on, all the time shivering like one of those jointed stick dolls. I had a thought I should put my arms around her, but I didn't do it.

"What went on back there? I could see, but I couldn't hear. Why did Peanuts hit Bobby?"

"It's complicated," I said. "I can't tell you right now. I gotta go with those guys again. It's going to take some time to get it straightened out."

"You mean right now?"

"I gotta."

"Men," she said, and shook her head. "There's no way you can understand them."

"Lori, I'm sorry. I'm just caught up in something and I can't quit right now."

"I'm only kidding," she said. "But tell me one thing: Did Peanuts admit it?"

"He didn't do it."

116

'Bobby Johns! '

"I can't say who did it. Not right now. It's complicated."

"Oh, for God's sake!" And then she started to laugh. "Go on! Go with those other goofs. I can see you're going to be up half the night trying to uncomplicate it."

"You're okay, Lori."

"Sure I am."

"You're more than okay, you're . . . ."

"Now don't get extravagant. Go take care of your business."

I got out of the car, closed the door. She lifted a hand to me and was gone; and I stood there, looking at a hole in the air, feeling the chill now, and wondering if anything in my life would ever be simple again.

"I'm not nuts," Peanuts said as I climbed into his car. Bobby Johns was sitting in the back. "I'm impulsive and compulsive and irresponsible and overaggressive, with strong anti-social tendencies, but I am probably not a true sociopath. Now that's right out of a psychiatrist's report. Cost my old man a thousand bucks to find out. He thought I might be nuts, too."

"You are nuts," Bobby Johns said from the back seat.

"I'm crazy, but I'm not nuts. There's a difference. Ask ole Marshie, here. Betcha he knows the difference."

"I know one thing. You keep calling me Marshie and it's gonna turn into a bad night for one of us."

"Right. Bein' nasty gets to be a habit."

I looked over at him. He was watching the road, his face serious for a change. I noticed his driving was controlled. I had expected him to burn rubber and show off, but he drove like a pro, very smooth.

"Hey, Peanuts, you're not really gonna take me down to jail, are ya?"

"I told you, it's up to Delaney. He's the dude you framed."

"I only did it because I thought it'd be a favor to you."

"Like I always told you, it don't pay to do favors for people."

"Will you quit kiddin'? This ain't funny."

"Well, you know what my dad always says."

"What?"

"You should have thought of that before you did it."

"Oh, for Christ sake!"

"You better talk to Delaney here. He's got your life in the palm of his hand."

"He ain't gonna help me. I know that." Silence for a long minute. "I don't see how you can turn against me this way."

"You sound like somebody in a soap opera."

"Boy, you are a mean son of a bitch, aren't ya?"

"Better slow down or you'll be goin' to jail with a broken nose."

And, you know, listening to them, I couldn't tell if Peanuts was serious. Would he send his friend to jail just to help *me* out? Or was he doing it to clear his own reputation? I couldn't buy that, either.

Actually, though, there was no question of Bobby going to jail. Not if it was up to me, anyway. I didn't know if that made me a bad citizen or not, but I wasn't ready to send some other guy to jail. Not for breaking into a school. And I wasn't going to send him to jail for trying to frame me.

"Well. . . ." Bobby Johns began, and then choked on his words. He finally got it out. "What do you say, Delaney? Are you gonna give me a break?"

I was tempted for an instant to keep him hanging, make him suffer. After all, this bird owed me.

"Nah, I'm not gonna turn you in."

"Hey, you mean it?"

"Of course, I mean it."

"Hey, Delaney, you're all right, you know that?"

"No, don't get me wrong. I'm not doing it because I'm a good guy. I'm doing it for myself."

"Yeah? Well, I don't get it, but I'm gonna say thanks anyway."

Peanuts drove silently. I was looking at three or four things inside my own head. It was like coming out under the open sky after being in a big tent for a long time. And the funny thing was that in some ways nothing had changed. The ghost of my cap would be hanging around the principal's office forever. And it didn't matter anymore. That was the amazing part.

"You probably won't believe this," Bobby Johns said. "But I've felt lousy ever since I did that."

"Oh, Bobby," Peanuts said. "You're gonna have me cryin' in a minute."

"You got no feelings, Peanuts."

"I been thinkin'," Peanuts said, with a big yawn. "Maybe I oughta turn you in. The case wouldn't stand up in court, but at least old man Williams will know who the guilty party is."

"You wouldn't do that!"

"I might. What do you think, Delaney?"

"Nah. You'd just feel rotten in the morning."

Peanuts laughed. "You want to go home, Bobby?"

"Yeah, I think that's what I'll do. Maybe get up early and go to church in the morning."

"Good idea." They both laughed. I felt another flicker of doubt. Had I been gamed? But what the hell, it didn't matter. The end result would have been the same, anyway.

"You know something, Delaney?" Bobby Johns said, as Peanuts pulled up in front of a dark house on a dark street. "Peanuts didn't know we weren't gonna block for you in that Millersville game."

"Cut it out, Bobby!" Peanuts sounded embarrassed.

He didn't even catch on till the half was almost over.
Bobby got out and slammed the car door and disappeared
around the corner of the darkened house.

"Is he telling the truth?"

"More or less. What difference does it make?"

"It makes a lot of difference. Why'd you let Foss think
it was you?"

"I didn't exactly let him think that," Peanuts said. For
once he wasn't laughing. "But I don't know, I'd put myself in a bind. Things get away from you sometimes. You
know what I mean?"

Yeah, I knew what he meant. I was trying to remember
exactly what had happened in the locker room that day,
but the details were foggy.

Peanuts put the car in gear and moved out into the street
again.

"Where d'ya want to go?"

"Home, I guess."

"Want to drink a beer first?"

"Sounds like a good idea."

He pulled right into the curb, reached under his seat,
and came up with two cans. They were still cold. I hesitated a second. "Don't worry about it," he said. "In this
town nobody cares where you drink beer as long as you
don't throw the cans on their porch."

I took a long swallow. It tasted good. As I said before, I
had always steered clear of booze because of what it did to
my father. But I had a sudden sure feeling I didn't have
to be scared of it. I wasn't my father, and I'd have to find

out for myself what was good for me and what was not.

"Was that Lori Curtin who brought you out to Harley's?"

"Yeah."

"You goin' out with her now?"

"Not exactly."

"What happened to that girl you had at the dance?"

"Nothing.'

"She looked like a winner. Lori's nice, too, though. And I'll tell you something else: Don't pay any attention to any cracks you might hear guys make about her. They're just wishin', that's all. Lori's her own woman."

"I know that."

He gave me a look. "You gonna see her again?"

"I don't know. Why the quiz?"

"'Cause I'm jealous, that's why. Lori and I were getting along good for a while, but then I started acting like a jerk, so she started treating me like one."

"Yeah? Well, we're just good friends, that's all." I didn't know why I was telling him that. I did know it was true, though. Ever since the kiss. I didn't know much about girls, but I did know one thing. You felt something happening or you didn't. Lori knew it, too, I was sure of that. We were going to be good friends. First time in my life I'd ever had a girl for a good friend.

"You know, I've been an awful jerk," Peanuts said.

"How's that?" I still didn't quite trust him. I knew now that I'd been wrong about some things, but that didn't mean I was ready to swallow any instant total reform baloney.

"I been thinkin' about it for a month or so. I never knew what a good thing I had going with Lori till I lost it."

"You sound like a songwriter."

"No, I'm not kidding you. Lori was the one person I could really talk to. I don't know why I had to screw up."

I didn't say anything. I was thinking about how you give a dog a bad name, and so on. Only this dog had given himself the bad name.

"Did she say anything about me?"

"She mentioned you a time or two."

"Yeah." He shook his head. "I must sound like a sixth-grader, right?"

"You want me to tell you what you sound like?"

He gave me a quick look. "Go ahead."

"You sound like a guy who's hurtin'."

He didn't reply. Just stared out through the windshield.

"Why did you give me such a hard time in the beginning?"

"I don't know. I thought you were putting me down . . . no. . . ." He shrugged and shook his head. "I get all caught up in my own act . . . think I gotta be number one." A long silence. "Sometimes I honest-to-God don't know *why* I act like I do."

I finished my beer, put the can under the seat.

"Want another one?"

"No. I probably shouldn't tell you this, but Lori said she always had hopes for you."

"She did? What kind of hopes?"

"Just hopes, I guess. That you'd make some changes."

He was scowling. Then his expression lightened, and he nodded to himself about something.

"Tell me one thing—were you going to back me up if I'd taken Bobby Johns to the cops?"

"I didn't think you would." He straightened in his seat. "You still headin' home?"

"No, I changed my mind. You know where Linda Gerhardt lives?"

"Sure. For a new guy you get around."

"Nah, she's having a party. I was invited, so I guess I'll drop in for a minute."

"I've never been invited to one of her parties," he said

as he pulled away from the curb. "I invited her and Benny to one of mine once, but they didn't come."

Linda's house was on the other side of town. Peanuts wheeled the Audi smoothly through the dark quiet streets. Holbrook sure wasn't any wild Saturday night town. But I knew that in lots of those houses people were gathered together for little Saturday night celebrations. Of course, you had to have some friends first. All of a sudden, I was feeling like a very lucky guy.

"You know what I been thinkin'," Peanuts said as he stopped in front of Linda's house. "I'd like to get back on the football team. I been working out every day. I'm still in shape."

"Yeah? Well, why don't you ask Foss? I don't think he's a guy who holds grudges."

"I know. But it's hard to ask him. I mean after what I did to the team and all. And what I said to him."

"It won't be easy. I don't mind telling you, I thought you were some kind of a psycho."

He nodded and looked at me. "I think I was sort of nuts back then. And I was poppin' a few pills. But that's no excuse, is it?"

I shrugged.

"Well . . . I don't know if it'll do any good, but I'm sorry I went after you like that."

"It does some good. I won't say I know where you're at, Peanuts, but I'll tell you what—if you want me to, I'll go with you. I mean we could go to Foss together, tell him bygones are bygones or however the hell you say it."

"Hey, that'd be good." He stuck out his hand. I shook it. "Maybe I could bring a couple of the other guys back, too. You're gonna need all the help you can get against Columbus next Saturday."

"That reminds me, do you know anything about Corwin Williams? What makes him an expert on football?"

"I didn't know he was an expert on anything."

I got out of the car. "See you Monday."

Peanuts nodded and moved off.

I moved toward the front door of the Gerhardt house, feeling funny about showing up at this hour. Linda opened the door to my ring.

"Why, Jack! Come on in. We'd given up on you."

There weren't many people in the living room. Benny came over and gave me a big handshake, like he hadn't seen me in a month. "You're looking good," he said, eyeing me. "I was a little worried about you this afternoon, but you're looking a lot more relaxed."

"Thank you, doctor."

He leaned closer, lowered his voice. "Cindy's out in the kitchen. She . . . uh . . . she might not be in the best mood in the world."

"Because I didn't show?"

"Well. . . ." He was having a hard time with something. But then another guy, Jeremy Hayden, who was editor of the school paper, came over. Ordinarily I'd have been glad to talk with him. Right now, though, I had to see Cindy. So I broke loose and went out to the kitchen. And damned if it wasn't just like the last time. There was Cindy, talking to some guy I'd never seen before. She saw me as I came in. Her eyes widened, then she looked back at this other guy, then she looked back at me again and said, "Hello, Jack," in a flat voice.

"Hi!" God, she looked great! She had on a green velvet dress and her hair was different, sort of loose and wavy. This time I didn't fumble around with any chicken-salad sandwiches. I walked straight over to her.

So what she did was introduce me to the guy. I didn't even catch his name. I was looking at her, knowing more surely with every second that something was wrong. She wouldn't meet my eyes, kept sliding past them, kept turning back to what's-his-name. I didn't know what to do. I felt like somebody was pulling the whole kitchen floor out from under me.

I said, "Maybe I can talk to you later?"

She gave me a stiff smile that seemed to say, Don't bother. I turned around and went back to the living room. Grabbed Benny and took him off in a corner.

"What the hell's the matter with Cindy? She won't even talk to me."

"That's what I started to tell you." Benny tightened his lips and shook his head. "But I don't know what's going on with you, Jack, either."

"What's that mean?"

"Okay, here's what happened. I told Linda and Cindy that you weren't coming. I also told them I thought the pressure from the burglary thing was bothering you——" He stopped and held up his hand. "I know, I probably shouldn't have told them that, but I was worried about you and it seemed like a good idea to tell them. Anyway, Cindy was very understanding and sympathetic. She said she was going to call you up . . . if you didn't want to come to the party, she'd go meet you somewhere. And then here comes—well I won't say who, because they didn't mean any harm, I guess—but here comes this couple, and the first thing they did was tell everybody how they'd seen you and Lori Curtin heading out of town in this fancy car."

"Oh, no!"

"And then somebody else made a crack about Lori, and I looked over at Cindy and she was pale as snow."

"Oh, boy." I felt sick in my stomach. "It wasn't like that."

Benny lifted his shoulders. "You have to admit it didn't sound too good."

"I was all screwed up in my head. I can't even remember why I thought I couldn't come here. But going out with Lori . . . well, it didn't have to do with sex or anything. We're friends, that's all.''

Benny was looking at me with that sincere and real good-guy expression of his. I was suddenly aware that everything was very quiet. Looking over my shoulder, I saw that the seven or eight people in the living room were all staring at me and Benny. They immediately got busy talking to each other again.

Benny spread his hands. "Well, they all know. Or think they know. You can't blame them for being curious."

"I don't blame 'em for anything." I was starting to get mad. But who was I mad at?

"You have to try to understand Cindy's side, too. When you come drifting in here at eleven o'clock . . . well, she might think you're treating her like a late date or something."

Sure she would. Or something.

"Who's that guy she's with?"

"Just some guy. She doesn't even like him."

"I've gotta try to explain to her."

"From what I know about women, she may not be in the mood to listen."

"She's got to listen. I really *care* about her!"

"Wait a minute. Let's get Linda into this." He was back in a second, towing Linda along. At first she was cool, but after a while she started to believe me.

"You poor guy! How do you get into these things?"

"By being stupid. But I've got to make it right with Cindy. And I don't think she'll even talk to me."

Linda made a worried face. "She can freeze when she wants to. Look, let me talk to her first. It might help."

"Okay. Hey, thanks."

Linda patted my arm. "Now don't be so intense. It'll work out."

I saw Linda go out to the kitchen. Then the guy Cindy had been talking to came into the living room. Then about ten minutes later Linda came back into the living room. Then the other guy went back in the kitchen.

"She doesn't want to talk to you," Linda said. "I tried and tried, but she wouldn't listen. When she gets hurt she goes inside herself and closes a door."

"What should I do?"

"Wait. That's all you can do. She's a very special person, Jack, and sometimes you just have to lay back and wait till she works things out for herself."

"Yeah, but I don't want her thinkin' . . . well, thinkin' what she's thinkin'."

"Don't forget you've got friends on your side now. We won't let it get worse." She looked up at Benny. "Will we, honey?"

"You bet we won't! Linda's right, Jack. Tomorrow she'll be in a better mood. We'll make a *good* pitch for you."

"I appreciate it. I mean I really do appreciate it. But I've gotta make a pitch for myself."

"If you go banging on her door now," Linda said, "she'll just put three or four more locks on it. Believe me. I know that girl."

But I had to try. There was no way I could go home without trying. I went out to the kitchen. Cindy was standing by the sink. The other guy was sitting at the table, smoking a cigarette.

"Would you mind excusing us for a minute?" I said to him.

He glanced at Cindy. She gave a little shrug. He got up and left.

"Cindy, I want to tell you what happened."

She turned her back on me. I crossed the kitchen and took hold of her shoulders. They were rigid. She moved away a couple of steps, then turned to face me again. She didn't look angry, just cold and set.

"I don't want to hear it."

"You won't even give me a chance?"

"Tell me one thing. Were you out with another girl tonight?"

"Yes, but it's not like you. . . ."

"I suppose I'm too old-fashioned," she said in a thin voice I'd never heard from her before. "But you can't go out with another girl and then come to me."

"It wasn't *like* that! I know it looks rotten, but if you'll just listen. . . ."

"I don't want to hear it. Please. Just go."

She sounded like she was reading a line in an old play. But it wasn't funny. She was getting paler and paler. It scared me.

"Okay. For now I'll go. But I'm not giving up, and I'm not lying. And Cindy, I love you."

She turned away. I left the kitchen and went and found Linda. "I made it worse. Will you go out there and see if she's all right?"

"She'll be all right, Jack." Linda smiled, trying to give me hope. "If you're going to love Cindy you'll find out. She lives on her own levels. Sometimes she's hard to reach."

"Hard to reach? She hates me; she won't even listen."

"If she hated you she'd listen." Again Linda patted my arm. Motherly. Sisterly. Or, maybe best of all, friendly. But it didn't help much. If Cindy hated me she'd listen? I didn't know what that meant, and I didn't believe it, anyway.

Sunday was dull and lonely and disconnected from my life. Outside the weather was beautiful. Trees all red and gold and the air with a sweet smokey tang. But it only made me feel worse. Cold rain and dreary skies would have at least matched the way I felt inside.

Around noon I tried to call Cindy at Linda's house. Linda told me Cindy didn't want to talk to me. She told me to wait and take it easy—same old stuff.

I went for a walk, not wanting to meet anybody, slouching along, hands in jacket pockets, feeling nothing but a big emptiness inside me. It was hard to remember how good I had been feeling last night after the business with Peanuts and Bobby Johns. Man, if this was what you got for falling in love . . . And it wasn't even my fault. But, of course, in a way it was. If I hadn't gone out with Lori . . . If this, if that. "But if you hadn't gone out with Lori, you wouldn't have straightened out the mess with Peanuts." I must have said it out loud because an old lady walking in front of me turned her head and gave me a sharp look.

My aunt and uncle knew something was wrong—probably figured it was the burglary. They didn't ask direct questions, just tried to cheer me up. After supper we played three-handed rummy. Not the greatest card game in the world, but it did get me out of myself for a while and it was good medicine.

On Monday in school I met Peanuts in the hall after the last bell rang, and we raced to Mr. Foss's room to catch him before he headed for practice. He was sitting at his desk, correcting some papers. Peanuts laid it right out on the line, and I'll tell you something, he did a job of it. No weaseling around. Apologized first, didn't try to explain too much, and then asked if he could get back on the team.

The coach watched him all the time over the tops of the big horn-rims he wore for close work. When Peanuts was done, Mr. Foss took his glasses off, took a slow breath, let it out, looked at Peanuts, looked at me. His face was pulled tight. He started to talk. In short stumbling sentences he said how much he appreciated Peanuts coming to him, and something about me, and me and Peanuts, and a few of his favorite thoughts on what sports are all about.

But then he came to the point of the whole thing, and the point turned out to be sharper than a bee sting. "You can't play, Peanuts. I'm sorry, because I would like to see you play again. And after what you've done today, I think you deserve the chance to play again. But it can't be done. Don't you see?" He was pleading with us. "We've built a team out of the rags and tags that were left when you and your friends walked out, and I can't break that team up now. I don't want to talk about fair, but that's what it comes down to. Fair. It wouldn't be fair to the kids who've been playing their guts out these past few games. And, in fact, it might even ruin the team." He paused, took another long breath, shook his head. "It's a hell of a note!"

Peanuts just stood there. He didn't nod or even blink, so far as I could see.

"Tell you what," Foss said, his face easing back to its natural genial expression. "How'd you like to scrimmage against the varsity in practice? You're the best linebacker in school. You'd be doing us a hell of a favor."

Peanuts sort of grunted, "Huh!" Then he laughed and said, "Yeah. You're right. I get the picture. You're right about it." All his words running together very fast. "Sure, I'll scrimmage. Give this turkey some practice." He glanced at me, grinning, looking more like the old Peanuts, but with a difference. " 'Cause he ain't seen no linebackers till he sees what Columbus-Murdock's got waiting for him."

And that's the way it went. The rest of the guys were, as they say, dumbfounded when Peanuts sauntered into the locker room. Coach explained things quick, and everybody picked up quick. I don't say everybody believed it, but guys were coming over and shaking Peanuts's hand and slapping his back. It got sort of emotional, like the return of the prodigal.

We had a great practice. No heavy hitting on a Monday, but the team was clicking and meshing. Benny was throwing better than I'd ever seen him. He was learning how to scan the field and spot the open man. Foss had never before given him enough of a chance to learn.

Tuesday's practice started the same way. Though it was a gray chilly day, there was a warmth in all of us and we were having fun, even in the grass drills. Football practice was the one time I was able to forget for a little while about Cindy Farr.

"We're going to concentrate on our passing game the rest of the week," Coach anounced after the warm-up. "I know it's a big change for us, and no doubt risky, but that Columbus-Murdock defensive unit is death against a straight running attack."

"How come you know so much about 'em?" Jake Johnson asked. "You got scouts down there?"

"I've got one scout. He's seen them play. When he speaks, I listen."

"Who's that?" Benny was curious.

Foss turned and pointed to a man standing on the sidelines. I hadn't noticed him before. But people are always coming and going during a practice and you never do pay much attention.

"Hey, Corwin!" Foss called. "Would you come out here for a minute?"

Corwin Williams? Nobody else. The chief of police himself. He ambled slowly toward us, a tall lean figure who moved nice and easy for an old man—or a man of any age.

"Tell them something about Columbus-Murdock," Foss said. And there was a certain respect in his voice that didn't have anything to do with the old man being a cop.

Corwin Williams looked us over with his slightly pop-eyed gaze and then began to tell us something about

Columbus-Murdock. How they ran from a pro-set. How they cross-blocked. How their defense switched back and forth from a 4–5–2 zone to a 4–3 bump and run. Lots of technical stuff, and some of it over my head.

Benny Younger whistled. "You sound like the man who wrote the book. How come you know so much about football?"

"I used to play some."

Yeah, I was thinking. So he used to play some. But more likely he was a Monday morning quarterback. One of those football nuts who watch every game on TV and learn the lingo, so they can tell the guy sitting next to them, "See, his drop is too short. The tight end was open in the crease and he didn't have time to spot him!" And so on . . . you've heard them.

"You're going to have trouble running against them, Delaney," Corwin Williams said, almost like he was reading my mind. "They've got three linebackers who could make most college teams right now. And your offensive line isn't big enough."

"So we pass," Foss said, not looking that happy about it.

"No, you run and you run and you run. And Delaney's going to get himself half-killed and so's your fullback. But you keep banging away until they get caught in the rhythm. And then you pass. And when you throw the ball, you score a touch. No other way you can stay close."

We were all staring at him with our mouths open. Who the hell was this old geezer of a cop to be telling our coach how to play a football game?

"I'm going to show you a play that might even beat them," the old geezer said. "Post pattern. Oldest in the game. But if it's done to perfection it can't be stopped. The way Gary Collins used to do it for the Browns. Perfection, mind you."

Oh, no! I was thinking. Just when things were going

great for us, this armchair expert has to stick his nose in and start changing things. Why would Foss let him get away with it? But Foss had turned his back and was watching a flight of starlings wheeling against the gray sky.

"Let's try one," Corwin Williams said. "Delaney, you set up wide. Only one way to run this route. Full speed down the sidelines, no fancy moves, then at the ten-yard line you cut for the goalpost, still full speed, and I mean fast as you can fly. When you look over your shoulder the ball will be there, but the defender won't."

"Sounds good."

"You bet. Benny's got a slingshot. He can throw to a spot. All you need is practice."

Somebody snickered. I guess Corwin Williams didn't hear it.

We were at the thirty-yard line, which meant Benny would have to throw forty yards. But, what the hell, we might as well humor the man.

We lined up. On the "Hut!" I took off, straight down the line, cut at the ten, looked back, saw the ball coming. But it was a shade late and I had to slow down and wait for it.

"That's the way you *don't* do it," Corwin Williams said, as I trotted back. "That's the interception game. Don't look back till you're almost at the post."

Benny sighed. It echoed what we were all feeling. I looked over at Coach Foss again. This time he was watching us.

"Why don't you show them, Corwin?" Foss said. "That's the only way they're going to believe you."

"Yeah, man!" This from Jake Johnson, who had been left out of the play. "Show us how they did it in the good old days."

"On this play, Jake," Corwin Williams said, "you're the decoy. You're running fly patterns all day and your speed is going to get you double coverage. That's why the

133

ball goes to Jack. Not because he's a better catcher than you, just because he'll be able to get open easier."

Jake shrugged. What the old coot was saying made sense, but it was all theory. Anybody can invent the perfect play on paper. Execution is something else.

"You gonna show us, sheriff?" Jake said with a mocking grin. Maybe his days in Detroit had made him unfond of any kind of policeman.

"Why not." Corwin Williams took off his big leather coat, stepped up behind the center. "Jack, you're wide left, Jake wide right. Jake goes straight for the flag, Jack cuts for the post. On three." Damned if he didn't sound like a quarterback . . . or maybe just a chief of police. As I took my position, I saw that all other action on the field had stopped. Everybody was watching us.

Corwin Williams started his call: "Hut, *one*. . . ." On "three!" I took off, running like I wanted to set a new mark for the forty. Made my cut. Positively did not look back till two strides from the post, then turned my head, starting to grin because I knew the ball would be bouncing around somewhere near the twenty-yard line. Turned my head . . . and there was the ball, big and soft as a feather pillow, just sitting in the air one step ahead of me. I reached out and grabbed it. Easiest, sweetest catch I ever made in my life.

When I got back, everybody was standing in a stupor, staring at this chief of police, who was putting his coat back on.

"One more play," Coach Foss pleaded. And I mean *pleaded*. "Show Benny how to hit Jake on the quick hitch. We've never been able to get it right."

"Nothing to it," Corwin Williams said, tossing aside his coat again. "You go down five yards, Jake, fast. Pivot off your outside foot and angle straight back to me. The ball will hit you on your second step." He looked at Benny. "This is a three-yard drop. Release the ball when Jake takes his first step toward you, and you've got to zing it. We'll snap on the first sound."

"What d'ya mean?" Our center, Joe Greenwood, looked around at this new coach.

"That means the first sound the quarterback makes, you hand him the ball. Even if he coughs."

I just stood back and watched.

Quarterback Williams said, "Red!" The center gave him the ball. Jake sprinted—and from a standing start he was as fast as you can get—Corwin Williams dropped back three quick steps, Jake made a beautiful cut, Williams brought the ball back to his ear, and as Jake took the first step toward him, the old man fired—"Snap!"— like cracking a whip. The football hit Jake right in the numbers and bounced twenty feet in the air.

"Threw a little too hard," Buffalo Bill said. "You have to get used to it." Putting his coat on again, he nodded to Foss and turned back to Benny. "Work on the timing," he said. "Timing is what makes it go." He gave the rest of us a serious smile, lifted his hand, and ambled off the field.

"Who *is* that guy?" Jake said, scowling and rubbing his chest.

"Name's Corwin Williams," Foss said with a grin.

"How can he throw like that?" I said. "He didn't even warm up."

"He stays in shape. I imagine he warmed up before he got here."

"I mean who *is* he?" Jake said.

"Used to be backup quarterback for the Rams. Three years. Unfortunately he was playing behind a guy named Van Brocklin, so he never got much field time. And then one day when he did, one of the Chicago Bears' hatchet men took his knee apart. He never played another game."

"Are you kiddin' me?"

Foss shook his head. "I've been after him for ten years to help me with this team, but he wouldn't do it. Said it wouldn't be right. Never did quite understand his reasons."

"For the *Rams*?" I couldn't get it through my head. "So how come he's a cop?"

Foss shrugged. "Corwin told me once that he never learned anything in school except how to play football. So when the knee went, he came back home and got a job as a deputy sheriff. Whatever that means."

"But how come nobody ever talks about it? I mean he must have been pretty famous around here."

"It was a long time ago. People forget, take things for granted. I don't know."

"But I don't understand why my uncle didn't tell me. He's always sayin' Corwin Williams this and Corwin Williams that, but he never told me who he was."

Foss grinned. "Your uncle's got his ways. He probably decided you'd get more of a kick out of it if you found out on your own."

A kick, all right. A kick for all of us. We worked on those two plays, plus a few others we had never tightened up on, for the rest of the week. I had never practiced any single play this intensively, and it gave me my first knowledge of what you have to do if you want to approach perfection.

It stopped being fun after Wednesday. But we kept at it, from the fifteen, the twenty, the thirty. By Friday Benny and I had the timing down. To the split second. It was a beautiful feeling when I turned my head on the dead run and time after time found that big fat football hanging there like an apple for the plucking.

Corwin Williams showed up a couple of times, standing on the sidelines, watching. But he never approached us again, never said a word. Just watched a while and then drifted away.

"Why do you suppose he changed his mind about helping you?" I asked Foss on Friday, as we left the field. "I mean after all these years. Has he got something against Columbus-Murdock?''

Foss shook his head. "No. Corwin's always got his own reasons.'' He put a friendly hand on my shoulder. "Let's not worry about the reasons. Let's just go out and beat this super-team. It'll be the upset of the year . . . do a lot of good for all of us.''

I thought of Peanuts, who had been working his butt off all week. An upset wouldn't do much for him, but he had sure done a lot for us. Peanuts was like a different guy these days. I had never believed in quick changes, but something important had happened to Peanuts, and when you watched him and talked to him you had no choice except to believe it.

And now on Friday night all the practicing was over and we were tired and loose and ready. To beat Columbus-Murdock? I didn't know about that. They were ranked number two in the state. But we were ready to do a few things as well as we could possibly do them. We were ready to make our run. And that's as ready as you can get.

That week hadn't been all football, of course. On Wednesday night I couldn't stand my loneliness any more, so I got Cindy's number from Linda and called her home in Columbus. A woman answered, probably Cindy's mother. She had one of those smooth educated voices that you don't hear much in a town like Holbrook.

Then Cindy was on the line. As usual, I stumbled all over myself trying to get the first words out. She listened, without saying anything, while I tried to explain what my movie date with Lori had been all about. But the trouble was, it didn't make much sense, even to me while I was telling it. No matter how I sliced it, I *had* chosen to go to the movies with Lori rather than to Linda's party. And the psychological reasons, which for me were the root of the whole thing, didn't sound convincing when I tried to tell them to Cindy.

"I'm sure you had good reasons," she said when I finished. Her voice was flat and calm and a million miles away. "But I'm the way I am, and you're the way you are, and I don't think it'll do any good to keep talking about it."

"Cindy, wait a minute!"

"Maybe I'll see you at Linda's sometime. I have to run now."

She hung up on me. Being hung up on is no good. Being hung up on by the girl you're in love with is awful. First I was mad and then I was sick and then I spent the rest of the night trying to figure out how I'd managed to mess up the best thing that had ever happened to me.

It was still smothering me the next day. I didn't hear a word any of the teachers said all morning. At lunch I went to the cafeteria, took some spaghetti and meatballs I didn't want, and sat at a table with Jake and Peanuts. They were talking football. I stared at my spaghetti.

"Hey, man, are you sick?" Jake said.

"Why?"

"You're all drawn out. You're pale. And I asked you a question three times and you didn't even hear me."

"Yeah, well. . . ." I was going to pass it off, make some dumb joke or something. But then I flashed on a good thought. These guys were my friends. And I was hurting. If you couldn't go to your friends when you were hurting, then you were dooming yourself to a rotten, lonely, lousy life. To most people that probably wouldn't seem very startling; to me it was like what they call a revelation. Like coming out from under that tent again.

So I told them the whole story, leaving out only a few very private things.

"Man, you're in trouble!" Jake said. "I was in love once and my girl ditched me for a dude with a ten-speed bike. Course, I was only twelve at the time, but it took me a year to get over it."

"It's not funny, Jake."

"I know it's not," he said, sobering. "I just don't know what else to say. Honest to God, I've never really *been* in love. It must be a bitch."

"It can be the best thing there is," Peanuts said quietly. He looked at me. "You really go for this Cindy, right?"

"Yeah."

"Well. . . ." He shook his head. "I know this sounds funny coming from me, but one thing I've found out is that sometimes the best thing you can do is just hang in there and wait. I mean all this stuff about taking the bull by the horns and so on—it doesn't always work out."

Same song Linda had sung. And it did sound funny coming from him. It was like a lot of things I had been told and was now finding to be wrong. You couln't always win simply by giving that famous old hundred-and-ten percent.

But when I got in bed Friday night I found I couldn't sleep. Maybe part of it was night-before-the-game tension, but most of it was Cindy. So then I got mad and gave myself what Aunt Frieda would call a good talking-to. What was I, a lovesick simpleton? Was I going to let some mule-minded girl make my life miserable? Who the hell was Cindy Farr, anyway? There were plenty of other girls around. Et cetera and so on, for half an hour.

And still, thoughts of her kept running through my mind. Memories, pictures . . . like a videotape I couldn't shut off. I saw her again in her brown corduroy jacket, with the whale button, the way she had looked that first night at Linda's. And her face . . . the quick funny little smiles . . . then the seriousness, her huge eyes widening, her mouth losing all its tension, her lips slightly parting, still and soft and trusting.

The tape ran and ran until I jumped out of bed and went downstairs, through the dark quiet of the house to the kitchen. I opened the refrigerator door without turning on the lights. The refrigerator light almost blinded me. I drank a glass of milk and stood in the dark until I could see again. The tape was still running. Cindy at the dance. Cindy under the streetlight. Cindy's kiss. It was all we had ever done together, just kiss, but I could feel it still, all through me; and I thought that if by some miracle we slept together the rest of our lives, the memory of that kiss would never fade.

Slept together the rest of our lives! What kind of baloney was that? I put the glass in the sink and walked carefully back up the stairs. Even so, a few of them creaked. No sound from my aunt and uncle's room though. Slept together the rest of our lives. . . . I'd probably never even see her again, for God's sake! I got in bed, and I guess the tape broke, because the next thing I knew it was Saturday morning, sunny bright and full of football.

We had sausages and eggs and grapefruit and oatmeal for breakfast. Big meal and good for me. Aunt Frieda shook her head in disbelief when I ate three bowls of oatmeal, but Uncle Fred said, "Eat up, boy! Breakfast like that'll stick to your ribs all day." He was right. I knew I wouldn't want any lunch. By then the pre-game butterflies would be making their moves.

My aunt and uncle were going down to Columbus for the game, and so it seemed were half the other people in Holbrook. The phone started ringing about nine, friends of my aunt and uncle making plans to meet before and after. Uncle Fred came back from one call with his owly eyes wide open. "That was Sam Donalds—he's the mayor," he said in an aside to me. "Well, him and Wilbur Gilliam and their wives are goin' down and they invited us out to dinner afterward. What do you think of that?''

''It's no big thing,'' Aunt Frieda sniffed. ''Sam Donalds never impressed *me* all that much.''

''No, but Wilbur. He quit speakin' to me for a while. I got the notion he was blamin' the trouble—oh, well, I guess that's all water over the dam now.'' He wrinkled his forehead at me. ''There's a rumor you boys got some kind of secret weapon ready. You really think you got a chance against them city slickers?''

''Sure we got a chance. But I wouldn't bet the hardware store on it.''

I didn't get down to the school until almost ten, the time the bus was scheduled to leave. All the guys were sitting around in the locker room, looking at everything except each other. Everybody was tight, which could be a good sign or a bad sign. You couldn't tell until you got into the action. I looked for Peanuts. He wasn't there. I didn't blame him. Riding the bench in your street clothes was no way to spend a Saturday afternoon.

Jake, Benny, and Kevin Torrance, and I sat together on the trip to Columbus. We didn't talk much. Mostly just stared out the windows at the rolling farmland. And stared inside ourselves at our own private little screens. I didn't let the Cindy tape roll. Instead I looked at some old ones. Me on the streets of Cleveland. Thirteen years old, forty or fifty dollars in my pocket, swaggering around . . . not like the tough nut I thought I was, but like the nutty punk I really was.

The tape went out of focus. I turned my head to look straight out the window. Everything was out of focus. It took a while to get clear again. I should have known better than to run *that* tape. Even the Cindy tape wasn't as bad as that one.

We finally reached the Columbus-Murdock school,

which turned out to be one of those old city high schools. It was a big square brick building with fancy columns and about a hundred steps in front. The stadium was in back. A real stadium. Must have held at least ten thousand. I didn't know there was any high school anywhere with a stadium like that. But, of course, I hadn't seen all that many high schools, either.

Coach didn't have much to say in the locker room. Nobody did. But the tightness was easing, and we were looking at each other again. Every now and then somebody would grin and somebody else would let out a strangled snort of a laugh, and all of a sudden everything was loose and we were clapping our hands and hollering. You could feel the energy that had been building all week. We might still get the wind kicked out of us, no guarantees on that. But we were going to play some ball, no doubt about that.

Coach Foss didn't give his regular pep talk. Just before we went on the field, he gathered us around and said, "Benny's going to call this game. All of it. I might send in a play now and then, but it will only be a suggestion. You can run it, Benny, or you can run whatever you think is best. Do you understand me?"

"Yes, sir."

"Maybe it's not the way to coach the biggest game some of you boys will ever play in. But, then again, maybe it is." He grinned at us. And, I swear to God, right then if he'd asked us to run through a brick wall, we'd have done our damnedest.

We won the toss, and on our first series Benny called three straight running plays. It was a little worse than trying to go through a brick wall because this wall had a way of moving and falling on you before you got started. Their line had ours outweighed by about twenty pounds a man. And they were fast and tough and smart. Their linebackers should have been playing for Notre Dame. That's the way it felt the first two times I got hit.

I was still the only punter we had and—never mind what Corwin Williams told my uncle Fred—punting wasn't one of the things I did best. The snap was a little low. I hurried and shanked it. Damn! And then a piece of the brick wall fell on me. When I picked myself up, the ref was walking off a fifteen-yard roughing-the-kicker penalty. That's the kind of thing that can turn a ball game around. Instead of Columbus having possession on our forty, it was still our ball, first and ten, almost at midfield.

Benny stuck to his game plan. Torrance on a slant for three hard ones. Me on a sweep for three more. And then, on third and four, he sent Jake deep to the flag. I was secondary receiver on this one, but I knew Benny would try to hit Jake, or at least make it look that way. Columbus-Murdock had the word on Jake Johnson. Their cornerback and the free safety were covering him. Although Jake beat them both for an instant, Benny threw the ball over all three outstretched pairs of arms and just out of bounds.

Punt formation. This time the snap was perfect and I got off a good high kick. Fair catch on the Columbus fifteen. And now the pounding started. They ran most of their plays from a pro-set formation. Nothing too fancy. Their backs were big and fast, their offensive line was really firing out, and they were able to move us. Move us, but not destroy us. Our defense was playing way over its head. Jeff Wagner and Kevin Torrance were hitting like locomotives. Most of the time I had to lay back, not getting in on too many tackles. I knew that sooner or later they'd throw. Their wide receiver kept running at me, and sometimes by me. He was good—very quick and very tricky. I'd never really learned to play cornerback, and this past week I hadn't had time to practice much with the defensive unit. So we were vulnerable; I knew it, and by now I was pretty sure Columbus knew it, too.

They made a first down. Then another. Grinding out the yards, using lots of minutes. It was third and two at our forty-seven. Our line dug in for the rush. But I knew what was going to happen. In my bones I knew it. The wide receiver came straight at me again. Their quarterback faked twice to his running backs, then rolled out. Play-action pass! The wide receiver gave me a head fake. Beautiful. Turned me just enough to lose me, and then he went by me like the well-known rabbit. I saw the ball arching over my head, felt sick . . . and then saw Jake Johnson sprinting . . . leaping . . . intercepting. Jake was taking care of me and taking care of the team. He was some kind of football player. I knew right then that in years to come I'd be telling people I knew Jake Johnson, way back when.

So back we went to it. Torrance up the middle, me on the sweeps. Nothing but pound, slice, take your lumps. Then I slipped through a nice hole for twelve more, and all of a sudden we had the ball first and ten on their thirty, and it was time for the big one. We weren't going to get many chances. We all knew that. We were going to get more tired as the game went on. Too many guys playing both ways. Columbus would get comparatively stronger.

Benny called the post pattern. First down. You could argue either way. But it was Benny's call, and nobody argued. I lined up wide, which I'd been doing occasionally all through the quarter. Only this time I lit the main burner. Straight down the sideline, their cornerback racing with me, then cut at the ten, off my right foot, best cut I ever made. Flying for the post. Two strides out, looked back . . . and there was the apple . . . just like in practice. I picked it lovingly and we had our first six points.

The quarter ended. In the second quarter Columbus had possession of the ball twelve minutes out of the fifteen.

144

They must have gained three hundred yards. And scored twice. Missed the conversion on the last one. The score was 13–7, their favor. My body was hurting. We were all hurting. We were out of our class. We knew it now if we hadn't known it before. Yet it made no difference. We would play this brutal game down to whatever its end might be.

I looked up and caught Jake Johnson studying me with some concern. He gave me a slow, somber smile. I nodded and said a silent, Yeah! We were thinking the same, all of us, and as we trotted toward the passageway that led under the stands to the locker room I could feel it coming out of each one of us and rising and forming a cloud, a kind of shield around us. We would play the rest of this game and we would do the best that was in us . . . and—the feeling was there—we still weren't ready to settle for just being close.

As we reached the entrance to the tunnel, I heard somebody call my name.

"Hey, Delaney! Hey, you, Jack Delaney!"

I looked up. A lot of people were leaning over the rail around the tunnel entrance. But I saw Peanuts, the flash of light on his long blond hair, the big square grin splitting that all-American-boy face of his.

"Come here!"

I glanced at the coach. He was already in the tunnel. I left the team and stepped over to the wall where Peanuts was. I had to look almost straight up. The way the stadium was built, even when Peanuts leaned over the rail he was still four or five feet above the top of my head.

Down at the other end of the field a band started to play. Peanuts said something.

"I can't hear you!"

"I said there's somebody here who wants to talk to you."

Peanuts disappeared. Another face loomed above me.

Huge brown eyes. Swinging black hair. The quick funny little smile.

"Cindy!"

"Hi, Jack." Though the band was still playing, Cindy's voice came through it, above or below, I don't know. And she wasn't even hollering.

"Lori's here, too," she said. "They came to my house this morning and they told me . . . they told me about twenty times before I would listen. They are really your good friends, Jack."

"I know."

"Oh, listen to me, explaining!" She was looking at me all serious and wondering. The smile came and went. And I knew she was unsure of herself and shy. "I'm going to drive up to Holbrook tonight, to Linda's. Do you want to ride with me?"

I nodded.

"I'm sorry for the way I acted," she said.

I waved it away with my hand.

"*Delaney!*" A voice called from inside the tunnel.

"I'll wait for you in front of the school," she said.

I nodded, six or eight times I guess, and then turned and went into the tunnel.

Winning. Losing. Getting what you wanted, or not getting it. Maybe things really did just happen when it was time for them to happen.

Like that football game. We won in the last four seconds. Torrance on a blast straight over center. We could have lost it just as easy. But it wouldn't have mattered. We'd have won anyway.

F
M   McKay, Robert

           The running back

     18348

                              16,397

F
M   McKay, Robert

           The running back

     18348

                              16,397

DATE	BORROWER'S NAME	
OCT 2 1985	Jim Sheroy "	314A
OCT 16 1985	renew	
OCT 23 1985	n Shermu	